Contents

An overview of our books for older, catch-up readers

The Magic Belt, Totem and Talisman 1 & 2 Series are four phonic reading series for older, 'catch-up' students. Starting at the very beginning, the reader is swept along with Zak's adventures while learning to read, following step-by-step phonic progression. The table below shows the over-arching structure of the four series and how they interlink.

Series	Suitable for	Reading level	Who is it aimed at?	What does it cover?
Introductory Workbook	Readers aged 8-14	KS1	Absolute beginners. Students with shaky knowledge of the sounds and letters of the alphabet, who would benefit from starting a phonics program from the very beginning	Sounds and letters of the alphabet within CVC words
The Magic Belt reading series (12 books) and workbook	Readers aged 8-14	KS1	Students with prior knowledge of the sound and letters of the alphabet	VCC, CVCC, CCVC, CCVCC words and consonant digraphs ch, sh, th, ck, ng, wh, qu, and suffixes −ed and −ing
The Totem reading series (12 books) and workbook	Readers aged 8-14	KS1	Students able to read a simple text at CVC level and who know most of the consonant digraphs but have poor knowledge of vowel digraphs	A re-cap of words from CVCC level all the way to CCVCC level and of the consonant digraphs. Introduction of alternative spellings for vowel sounds, e.g. the spellings <ai, ay, ai and a> for the sound 'ae'
Talisman 1 Series (10 books) and workbook	Readers aged 8-14	KS1	Students who have poor knowledge of the phonic code and alternative spellings for vowel sounds	Re-cap of alternative spellings covered in the Totem Series and additional alternative spellings for new vowel sounds
Talisman 2 Series (10 books) and workbook	Readers aged 8-14	KS1/KS2	Students who have gaps in the their knowledge of the phonic code	More complex alternative spellings for vowel and consonant sounds and suffixes

Notes on the Talisman Series and Workbook

Talisman Series

Introduction
The Talisman Series is aimed at older students who need to learn the Phonic Code in order to make progress in their reading. The books introduce the vowel sounds and their alternative spellings. The series includes 10 books, each with a phonic or spelling focus. This workbook, based on the stories, includes a variety of activities which teach and consolidate an understanding of the Phonic Code.

Order of the books
The Talisman Readers can be read out of order, but the storyline works better if they are read in the numbered sequence.

Pronunciation
At the beginning of each book, there is a word list to help the reader learn the alternative spellings of vowel sounds in the English Phonic Code. Pronunciation of some sounds may vary, according to regional accents. The word lists may not always match the pronunciation of the student. This point should be discussed and the lists adapted to the student.

Blending not guessing
Students should be encouraged to blend the sounds into words. If there are spellings they do not know, point to the part of the word that is new and tell them the sound. Then get the student to blend the sounds into the word.

Use precise pronunciation
When blending sounds together, say the consonants without the added 'uh' sound, e.g. 'c' 'a' 't' not 'cuh' 'a' 'tuh'.

Teaching alternative spellings
The English Phonic Code is complex. This series presents up to 7 alternative spellings for a vowel sound. The teacher may need to introduce these spellings gradually if the student has difficulty learning all the alternative spellings at a time.

Splitting multisyllabic words
It is important to teach students how to split multisyllabic words. This will enable them to use successful and independent strategies when reading and spelling long words. There are a number of approaches to splitting multisyllabic words depending on the teaching method:
- A spelling rules approach, e.g. the doubling rule: s i t / t i ng
- A phonic approach which maintains phoneme/grapheme fidelity, e.g. s i tt / i ng
- A morpheme approach which emphasizes the meaning of parts of the word: l i f t /ed
This workbook allows the teacher to use any method he/she is teaching the student.

New vocabulary
Each new book offers an opportunity to learn new vocabulary on the 'Vocabulary' page. This page explains the words as they appear in the context of the text. The teacher may wish to discuss additional meanings of the word with the student.

The Workbook

This workbook complements the Talisman Series. Ten chapters in the workbook correlate to the 10 books in the series. Each chapter offers activities based on the phonic focus of each of the books. Before reading the books, students would benefit from practicing word building, blending, reading and sorting activities. These activities feature at the beginning of every chapter. Follow-up activities, such as comprehension, spelling and various games, should be used after reading the texts. The teacher can select from the activities in each chapter to maintain interest and variety.

The chapters for Books 2, 5, 6 and 10 include a sorting activity for a spelling that represents different sounds. These activities teach the student that he/she may need to try an alternative sound when reading certain graphemes, e.g. <ea> represents different sounds in: br'ea'k, t'ea'm and h'ea'd.

An instruction for every activity in the workbook appears at the bottom of each page.

Phonic sequence in the Talisman Series: Books 1–10

Book	Title	Phonic focus	Spellings
1	The Talisman	'ae'	ay, ai, a, a-e, ea, ey
2	Stampede!	'ee'	ee, ea, y, e, ie, e-e, ei
3	Shadow in the River	'oe'	ow, oa, oe, o-e, o
4	Deep Sea Danger	er, ir, ur, or ear	er, ir, ur, or, ear
5	Hounded in the Snow	'ow' and 'oi'	ow, ou & oy, oi
6	Death at Noon	'oo'	oo, ue, u-e, ew, ou, u
7	A Cry in the Dark	'ie'	igh, ie, i-e, i, y
8	Attack at Nightfall	'aw'	aw, awe, a, al, au, ough
9	Mountain Scare	air, are, ear, ere, eir	air, are, ear, ere, eir
10	The Dark Master	ar	ar

Talisman Series Workbook

for Books 1-10

Name: _____

Students can use this page as a personalized front cover for their Talisman Series work.
They may wish to decorate each symbol in the talisman as they read the series.

Book 1: The Talisman

Questions for discussion

Chapter 1

   1. Why did Zak want to throw the talisman in the lake? (p. 2)

   2. What does 'The sky was ablaze with red' mean? (p. 3)

   3. Why does Zak say "A great end to a great day"? (p. 3)

Chapter 2

   1. What made Zak fall on the rocks? (p. 5)

   2. Zak felt 'a jolt of pain'. What does that mean? (p. 5)

   3. How did the talisman save Zak? (p. 9)

Chapter 3

   1. What does the troll want from Zak? (p. 10)

   2. Why do you think the troll has chains on his legs? (p. 10)

Chapter 4

   1. What is the strange thing that happens to Zak? (p. 12)

   2. What does Zak find out when he gets home? (p. 16)

   3. What did Zak feel when he read the note on the gate?

   (p. 16)

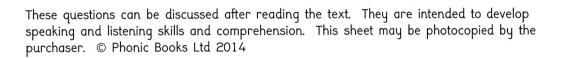

Book 1: Blending and segmenting: 'ae'

rain	r	ai	n		
they					
gate		a		e	
baby					
steak					
train					
plate					
prey					
spray					
snake					
breaking					
making					
fainted					

Blend the sounds into a word. Segment the word into sounds by writing one sound in each square. Split vowel spellings (a–e) are represented by half squares linked together. This sheet may be photocopied by the purchaser.   © Phonic Books Ltd 2014

Book 1: Reading and sorting words with 'ae' spellings

ai	ay	a	a-e	ea	ey

sale	able	they	faint
great	late	lazy	tray
nail	break	flame	angel
day	pain	steak	mate
David	stay	trail	gray
making	drain	whale	spray
strain	blame	pray	brain
stain	frame	baby	clay

Photocopy this page onto card and cut out the words. Read and sort the cards out according to the 'ae' headings at the top of the page. This sheet may be photocopied by the purchaser. © Phonic Books Ltd 2014

10

Book 1: Spelling: 'ae'

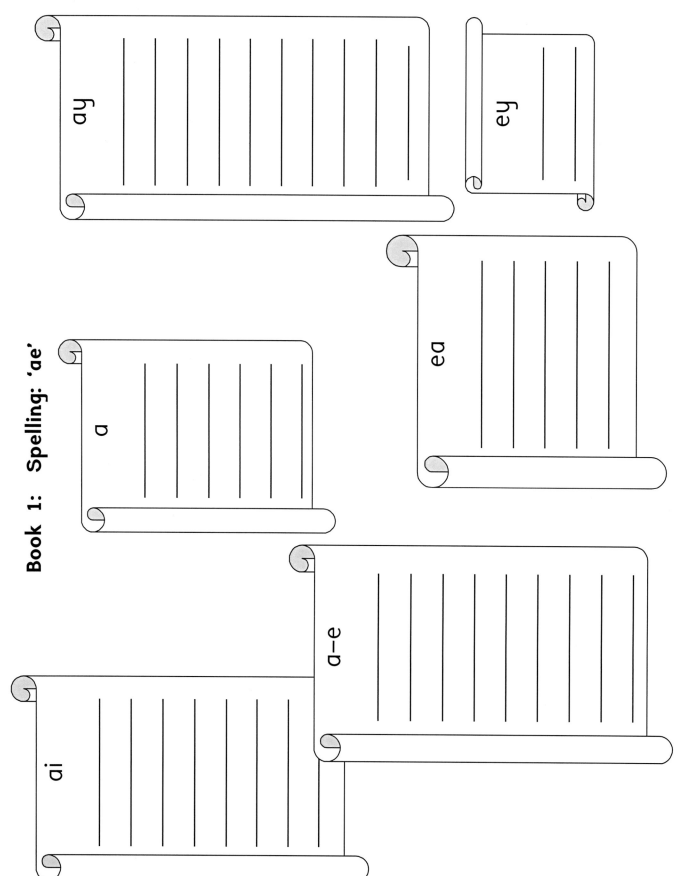

ay

ey

a

ea

ai

a–e

Read the text in Book 1, 'The Talisman'. Find the words with 'ae' spellings. List the words in the correct column. This sheet may be photocopied by the purchaser. © Phonic Books Ltd 2016.

Book 1: Reading and spelling

Zak went up the trail. It was a hot day. He sat in the

shade. The sheep grazed in the grass.

"This talisman is a fake. I'll break it. I'll chuck it in the

lake," he said, but something made him wait.

Z a k _ _ _ _   _ _   the

_ _ _ _ _ . _ _   was   _

_ _ _ _ _ .   He   _ _ _

_ _   the   _ _ _ _ .   The sheep

the

_ _ _ _ _ _   _ _

_ _ _ _ .

"This   _ _ _ _ _ _ _ _   _ _

a   _ _ _ _ . I'll   _ _ _ _ _   it.

I'll   _ _ _   it in the   _ _ _ _ ," he

said,   _ _ _   something   _ _ _ _

him   _ _ _ .

Copy the text in the top scroll to the bottom scroll. Write a sound on each line,
e.g. t r ai l. Where the vowel spelling is split (a–e), there is a link, e.g. sh a d e .
This activity can also be used for dictation.

Book 1: New words

Explain these words:

pelt – _____   daybreak – _____

jolt – _____   plains   – _____

scale – _____

talisman – _____

Link the sentences so that they make sense:

Zak ran to the cave because	Grandpa had been taken to the great plains.
When the lightning struck Zak,	the rain pelted down.
The note on the gate said that	he felt a jolt of pain.
When the troll swung his club,	"We will set off at daybreak!"
When the talisman began to glow,	into the lake.
When Zak found the note, he said,	Mim gazed at it.
Zak wanted to chuck the talisman	Zak scaled the tree.

Discuss the new words in the text and get the reader to explain them verbally and then in writing (the reader may need help with spelling). The reader can then match the two parts of the sentence.
This sheet may be photocopied by the purchaser. © Phonic Books Ltd 2014

Book 1: Comprehension 1

The troll – what's missing?

This troll is male. His name is Slobber. He has a crazy look of hate on his face. He has chains on his legs. He has long nails. He stinks. He has stale breath. He behaves in an angry way. He has a club in his hand. He raises it to slay his enemy. He obeys the Great Master.

Read the text above. Spot what is missing from the picture. Add it to the picture. For students who enjoy drawing, photocopy the text without the picture. Ask them to read the passage and draw a picture that fits the description. This sheet may be photocopied by the purchaser. © Phonic Books Ltd 2014

Book 1: Writing

The troll – what is he like?

stale breath

eyes full of hate

chains on his legs

waiting to slay his enemy

behaves in an angry way

long nails

raises his club

great, big hands

crazy look on his face

obeys the Great Master

sways as he walks

Describe the troll.

_____
_____
_____
_____
_____
_____

Describe the troll. You can use some of the words in the labels. This sheet may be photocopied by the purchaser. © Phonic Books Ltd 2014

Book 1: Comprehension 2

Trolls – true or false?

Trolls are scary creatures from Nordic fairy tales. In these tales, some trolls are big, ugly and savage. They can have tusks, a tail or one eye. Other trolls can be very small and live in big families. Trolls can also look like wild humans. They can be men or women. Trolls live under the ground in hills or in caves. In some tales, they can shape shift and change into a cat or a dog or a log or a tree. In the stories, trolls always steal. Sometimes they steal food from the table. Sometimes they will steal a new baby. They may leave a baby troll in the cradle in its place. People always blamed trolls for bringing bad luck.

Is it true?	yes	no
Trolls come from English fairy tales.	☐	☐
Trolls are always big and ugly.	☐	☐
Trolls live under the ground.	☐	☐
Some trolls can shape shift into a cat or a dog.	☐	☐
Trolls steal pots and pans.	☐	☐
People said trolls made bad things happen.	☐	☐

Read the text. Then read the sentences below and put a check in the boxes according to whether they are true or false. This sheet may be photocopied by the purchaser.

Book 1: Splitting two-syllable words with 'ae' spellings

apeman	ape	man	apeman
David			_____
afraid			_____
playmate			_____
payment			_____
baking			_____
breakneck			_____
greater			_____
shapeless			_____
checkmate			_____
aiming			_____
remain			_____
delay			_____

This activity allows the student to practice splitting two-syllable words. The teacher can use his/her own approach to splitting syllables (see page 3 for the different approaches to splitting words into syllables). These words can be used for dictation. This sheet may be photocopied by the purchaser.
© Phonic Books Ltd 2014

Book 1: Homophones 1: Which is which?

pail	pale

tale	tail

mail	male

steak	stake

whale	wail

great	grate

prey	pray

sail	sale

The student can draw an image on each card to help him/her remember the meaning of the word. Photocopy the cards and play 'Concentration'. Spread the cards face down and players take turns to find matching homophone pairs. This sheet may be photocopied by the purchaser.

Book 1: Homophones 2: Sail or sale?

1.   The boat had a _____.

2.   We went shopping. The _____ was on.

3.   I like to eat _____ and chips.

4.   I pushed the _____ into the ground.

5.   Mom told the kids a fairy _____.

6.   The dog wagged his _____.

7.   The mailman left the _____ on the mat.

8.   A girl is a female. A boy is a _____.

9.   The _____ is the biggest animal on earth.

10. To '_____' means to cry out loud.

11. A church is where some people gather to _____.

12. The lion jumped on its _____.

13. I like to _____ cheese on my pizza.

14. We had a _____ day at the fair.

15. Jack and Jill went to fetch a _____ of water.

16. When she saw the ghost, her face went _____.

| mail male | prey pray | steak stake | tail tale |
| great grate | whale wail | sail sale | pale pail |

Read the sentences above. The student can use the homophone cards from the previous page to select the correct homophone for each sentence. This sheet may be photocopied by the purchaser. © Phonic Books Ltd 2014

Book 1: Stepping stones game: 'ae'

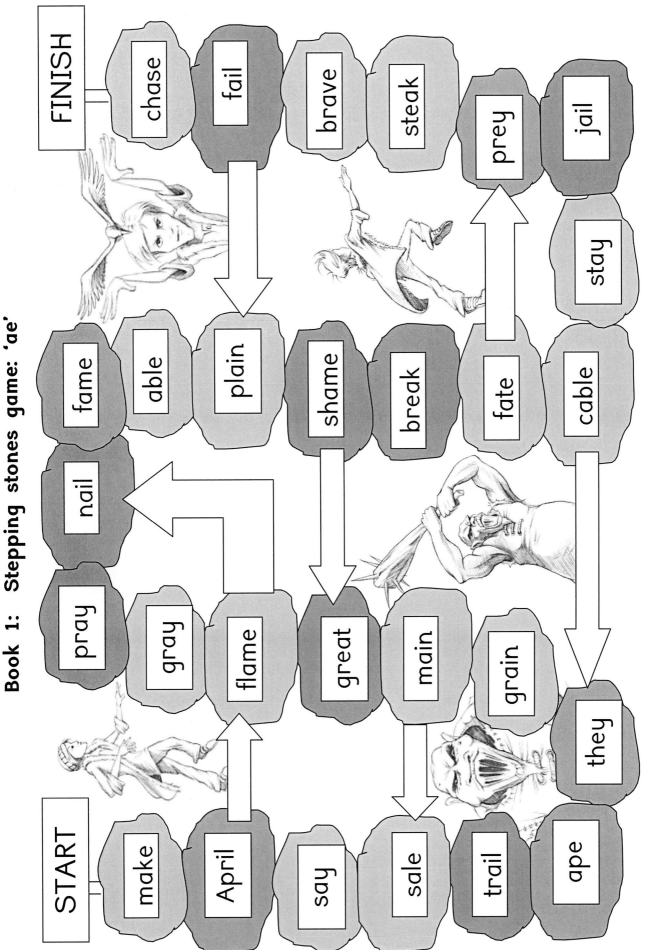

FINISH

chase · fail · brave · steak · prey · jail

fame · able · plain · shame · break · fate · prey · stay

pray · nail · gray · flame · great · main · grain · cable

START

make · April · say · sale · trail · ape · they

This game is for 1–4 players. Play with counters and die. This sheet may be photocopied by the purchaser. © Phonic Books Ltd 2014

Book 1: 4-in-a-row game: 'ae'

gray	gate	nail	acorn	tray
great	table	play	late	waist
break	stay	game	trail	cable
cake	David	prey	say	brain
faint	stray	steak	baby	same
aim	able	trail	tape	make
they	day	blame	wait	acorn

Play with two sets of colored counters. Two players take turns to read the word and put a counter on the word. The winner is the first to get four of his or her counters in a row. The winner places a counter on a talisman. The game is played four times until all the talismans are covered. This sheet may be photocopied by the purchaser. © Phonic Books Ltd 2014

Book 2:   Stampede!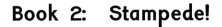

Questions for discussion

Chapter 1

   1. Why did Zak have a bad feeling? (p. 2)

   2. What is it like in the great plains? (p. 3)

Chapter 2

   1. Zak felt uneasy near the stream. Why? (p. 5)

   2. How did Zak and Mim know that Grandpa had been near the stream? (p. 6)

   3. Why do you think the button was in the stream? (p. 7)

Chapter 3

   1. Why did Zak leave Mim? (p. 8)

   2. Why do you think the horsemen seized Mim? (p. 10)

Chapter 4

   1. How did the talisman help Zak? (p. 11)

Chapter 5

   1. Why did the bull say "Don't be afraid!" to Mim? (p. 16)

These questions can be discussed after reading the text. They are intended to develop speaking and listening skills and comprehension. This sheet may be photocopied by the purchaser.

Book 2: Blending and segmenting: 'ee'

feel	f	ee	l		
each					
Pete		e		e	
she					
chief					
envy					
delete					
creep					
dream					
shriek					
angry					
began					
defeat					

Blend the sounds into a word. Segment the word into sounds by writing one sound in each square. Split vowel spellings (e–e) are represented by half squares linked together. This sheet may be photocopied by the purchaser. © Phonic Books Ltd 2014

Book 2: Reading and sorting words with 'ee' spellings

ee	ea	e	ie	ei	e-e	y

read	seem	she	field
seize	Pete	runny	messy
creep	sneak	belong	chief
receive	delete	relax	agree
stream	grief	compete	ceiling
indeed	hilly	release	repeat
stampede	shield	begin	scream
feeling	steal	complete	thief

24

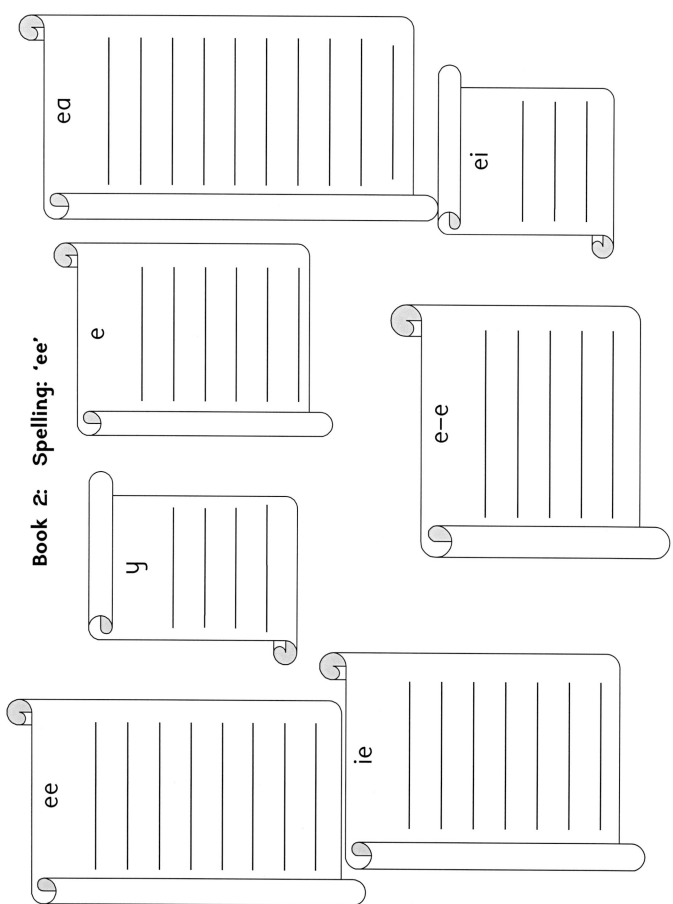

Book 2: Spelling: 'ee'

ea

ei

e

e–e

y

ie

ee

Read the text in Book 2, 'Stampede!'. Find the words with 'ee' spellings. List the words in the correct column.
This sheet may be photocopied by the purchaser. © Phonic Books Ltd 2014

Book 2: Reading and spelling

Zak and Mim came to a stream. Mim dipped her feet in the cool stream.

"It's freezing!" she shrieked. Zak had a creepy feeling.

Something seemed to be following him.

<u>Z</u> <u>a</u> <u>k</u> _ _ _   _ _ _

_ _ _ _ to _ _ _ _ _ _ _.

_ _ _ _ _ _ _ her _ _ _

_ _ the _ _ _ _ _ _ _ _ _.

"It's _ _ _ _ _ _!" she

_ _ _ _ _ _.

Zak _ _ _ a _ _ _ _ _

_ _ _ _ _. Something

_ _ _ _ _ to _ _ following

_ _ _.

Book 2: New words

Explain these words :

jagged – _____   seize – _____

stream – _____   plead – _____

uneasy – _____   retreat – _____

Link the sentences so that they make sense:

The jagged peaks	and almost crushed him.
Zak was uneasy because	reached up to the sky.
When the bull attacked,	she began to scream.
Mim found a green button	he felt someone was following him.
When the horseman seized Mim,	in the stream.
Zak pleaded with the talisman	the horsemen began to retreat.
The horseman reared up over Zak	to help him.

Discuss the new words in the text and get the reader to explain them verbally and then in writing (the reader may need help with spelling). The reader can then match the two parts of the sentence.
This sheet may be photocopied by the purchaser. © Phonic Books Ltd 2014

Book 2: Comprehension 1

The bull – what's missing?

When the horseman seized Mim, the bull got very angry.

His long horns could pierce his enemy and make him bleed.

He began to stamp his hooves. He ran at the horseman at

full speed. Then he stopped. Steam was coming out of

each nostril.

Read the text above. Spot what is missing from the picture. Add it to the picture. For students who enjoy drawing, photocopy the text without the picture. Ask them to read the passage and draw a picture that fits the description. This sheet may be photocopied by the purchaser. © Phonic Books Ltd 2014

2

Book 2: Writing

The three horsemen – what are they like?

half man, half horse

can stampede

are very strong

are defeated by the bull

retreat when the bull attacks them

have helmets

have breastplates

sweep Mim off her feet

are angry

obey the Great Master

demand the talisman

Describe the three horsemen.

_____

_____

_____

_____

_____

_____

_____

Book 2: Comprehension 2

Horsemen – true or false?

Horsemen are also called Centaurs. They come from Greek myths. The horseman is part man and part horse. A man grows from where the neck of the horse should be. No one knows the origin of the horseman in Greek mythology. Some people think that the idea of the horseman started when people first saw men riding horses. They thought that the men and the horses were attached. Horsemen can have two different natures. Some can be wild and untamed. In some stories, they are bad. Other horsemen can be sensible, like teachers. Horsemen represent the two different sides of a person: one wild, the other sensible.

Is it true?	yes	no
Horsemen come from Greek mythology.	☐	☐
Horsemen are part man and part dog.	☐	☐
A horseman has the body of a man and head of a horse.	☐	☐
Horsemen can be funny.	☐	☐
Horsemen are always bad in stories.	☐	☐
Some horsemen can be sensible and some can be wild.	☐	☐

Read the text. Now read the sentences below and put a check in the boxes according to whether they are true or false. This sheet may be photocopied by the purchaser. © Phonic Books Ltd 2014

Book 2: Splitting two-syllable words with 'ee' spellings

keeping	keep	ing	keeping
weaker			_____
compete			_____
belief			_____
creepy			_____
easy			_____
evil			_____
achieve			_____
ceiling			_____
agree			_____
beaten			_____
stampede			_____
relief			_____

This activity allows the student to practice splitting two-syllable words. The teacher can use his/her own approach to splitting syllables (see page 3 for the different approaches to splitting words into syllables). These words can be used for dictation. This sheet may be photocopied by the purchaser.
© Phonic Books Ltd 2014

Book 2:   Homophones 1: which is which?

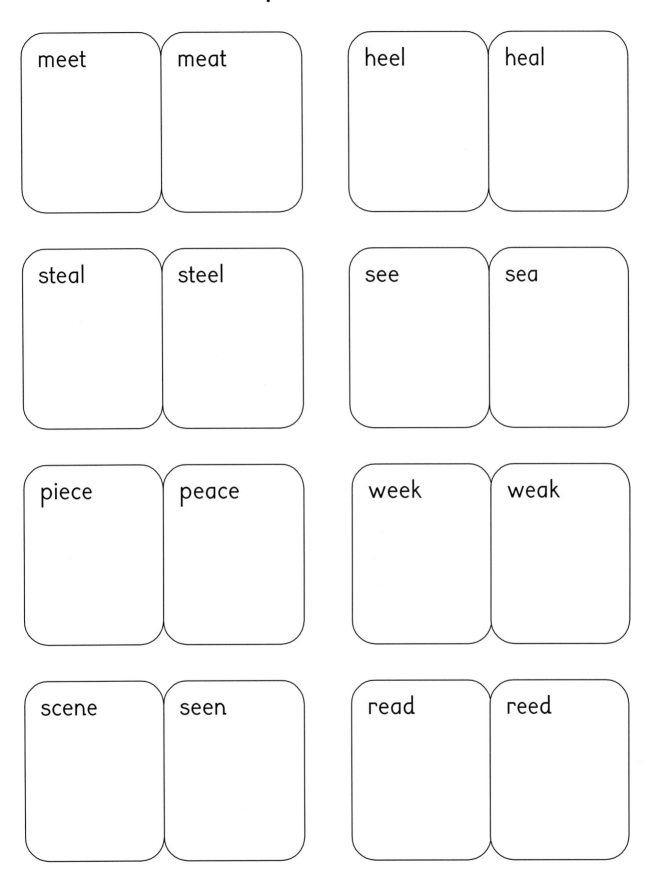

meet	meat
heel	heal
steal	steel
see	sea
piece	peace
week	weak
scene	seen
read	reed

The student can draw an image on each card to help him/her remember the meaning of the word.
Photocopy the cards and play 'Concentration'. Spread the cards face down and players take turns to
find matching homophone pairs. This sheet may be photocopied by the purchaser.

Book 2: Homophones 2: Week or weak?

1.   The school trip is next _____.

2.   When I was sick, I felt very _____.

3.   I like to eat _____.

4.   The kids _____ in the park after school.

5.   I _____ the paper every day.

6.   A _____ grows in rivers and ponds.

7.   The last _____ in the movie was really scary.

8.   I haven't _____ her for a week.

9.   The bridge is made of _____.

10.   To _____ is to take something that is not yours.

11.   Mom cut him a big _____ of cake.

12.   When there is no war, there is _____.

13.   The _____ is the back part of the foot.

14.   The cut on my hand will _____ in a week.

15.   Fish swim in the _____.

16.   We went to _____ a comedy last week.

read reed	meet meat	scene seen	heel heal
piece peace	week weak	sea see	steel steal

Read the sentences above. The student can use the homophone cards from the previous page to select the correct homophone for each sentence. This sheet may be photocopied by the purchaser. © Phonic Books Ltd 2014

Book 2: Stepping stones game: 'ee'

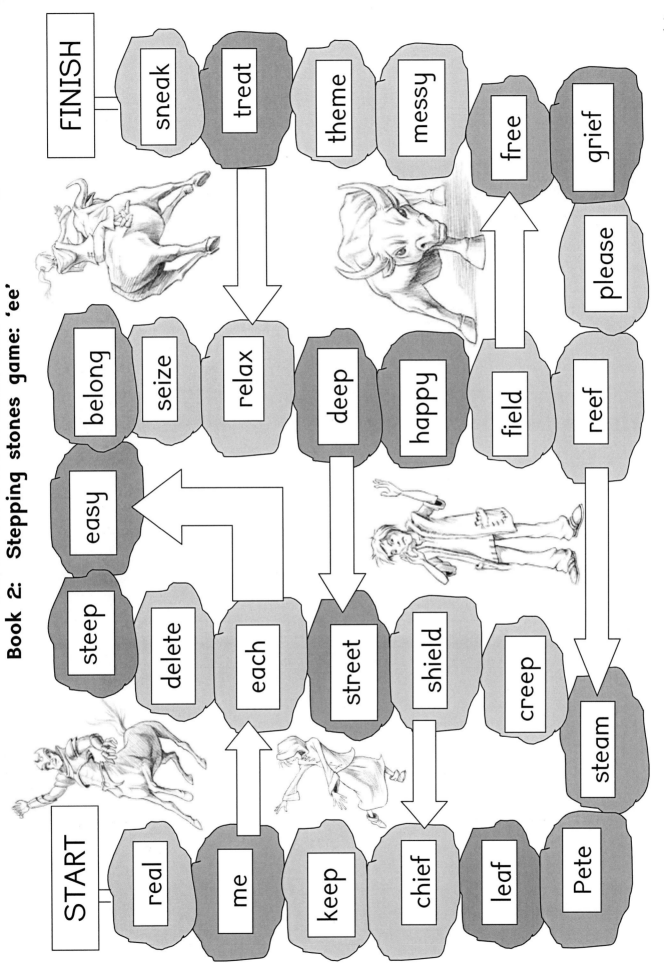

FINISH

sneak
treat
theme
messy
free
grief

belong
seize
relax
deep
happy
field
reef

easy
steep
delete
each
street
shield
creep
steam

START
real
me
keep
chief
leaf
please
Pete

33

This game is for 1–4 players. Play with counters and die. This sheet may be photocopied by the purchaser. © Phonic Books Ltd 2014

Book 2: 4-in-a-row game: 'ee'

free	eat	she	each	chief
grief	funny	reach	heel	delete
seize	leave	leek	begin	shriek
we	bleed	relief	shield	relax
trees	beans	badly	runny	field
steep	priest	piece	evil	breed
peach	greed	Keith	niece	sunny

Play with two sets of colored counters. Two players take turns to read the word and put a counter on the word. The winner is the first to get four of his or her counters in a row. The winner places a counter on a talisman. The game is played four times until all the talismans are covered. This sheet may be photocopied by the purchaser. © Phonic Books Ltd 2014

Book 2: Reading and sorting words with <ea> spelling

head	team	great

break	dead	lead	read
read	steak	bread	heal
dream	breakable	dreamt	ready
please	steady	cream	weapon
easy	heaven	dealt	steal
leave	feather	each	instead
heavy	meal	scream	health
wealth	heap	weak	dread

Photocopy this page onto card and cut out the words. Read and sort the cards out according to sounds of the <ea> spelling. The three sounds are: 'e', 'ee' and 'ae'. This sheet may be photocopied by the purchaser. © Phonic books Ltd 2014

Book 3: Shadow in the River

Questions for discussion

Chapter 1

    1. Where does this story take place? (p. 1)

    2. What does the word 'current' mean? (p. 3)

Chapter 2

    1. What do Zak and Mim find in the river? (p. 7)

Chapter 3

    1. What are 'rapids'? Explain how they are formed. (p. 8)

    2. What did Zak think the shadow in the river was? (p. 10)

Chapter 4

    1. What was the shadow in the river really? (p. 12)

    2. 'Long whiskers probed the riverbed.' What does that mean?

    (p. 13)

Chapter 5

    1. Why did the catfish attack Zak? (p. 14)

    2. Why do you think Zak turned into an otter? (p. 16)

38

Book 3:   Blending and segmenting: 'oe'

row	r	ow			
go	☐	☐			
hope	☐	o	☐	e	
toe	☐	☐			
most	☐	☐	☐	☐	
roast	☐	☐	☐	☐	
slope	☐	☐	☐	☐	☐
foe	☐	☐			
groan	☐	☐	☐	☐	
stone	☐	☐	☐	☐	☐
snowing	☐	☐	☐	☐	☐
floats	☐	☐	☐	☐	☐
joking	☐	☐	☐	☐	☐

Blend the sounds into a word. Segment the word into sounds by writing one sound in each square. Split vowel spellings (o–e) are represented by half squares linked together. This sheet may be photocopied by the purchaser. © Phonic Books Ltd 2014

Book 3: Reading and sorting words with 'oe' spellings

o	oa	ow	o-e	oe

rope	go	hole	bow
toe	bold	bone	coat
joke	most	pole	show
groan	hold	float	goes
snow	smoke	shoal	broken
roast	flow	goat	note
alone	toast	crow	close
know	soap	grope	hero

Photocopy this page onto card and cut out the words. Read and sort the cards out according to the 'oe' headings at the top of the page. This sheet may be photocopied by the purchaser. © Phonic Books Ltd 2014

40

Book 3: Spelling: 'oe'

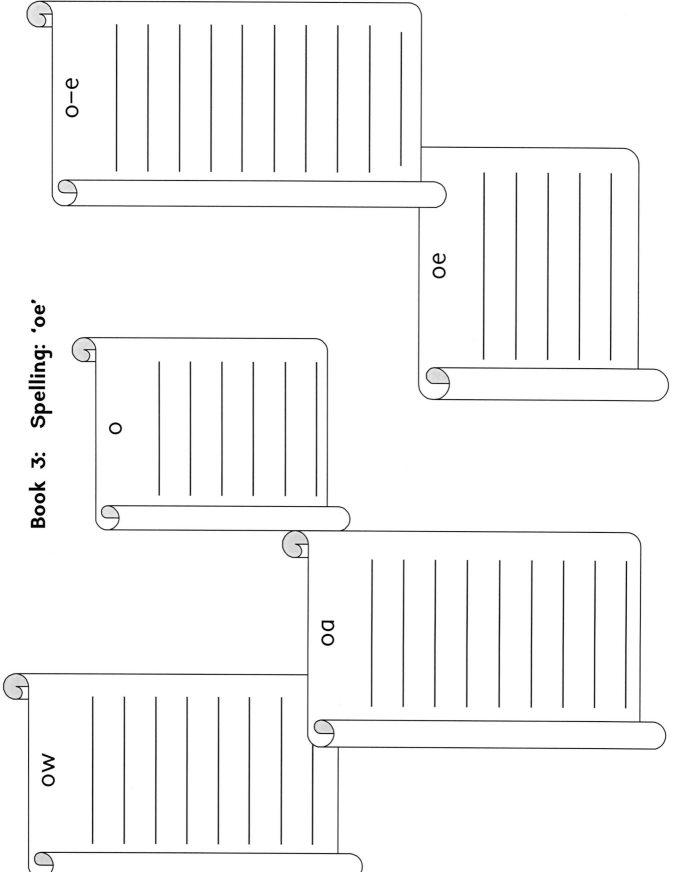

o–e

oe

o

oa

ow

Read the text in Book 3, 'Shadow in the River'. Find the words with 'oe' spellings. List the words in the correct column. This sheet may be photocopied by the purchaser. © Phonic Books Ltd 2014

Book 3: Reading and spelling

There were no holes in the boat. Zak and Mim jumped

in. They floated slowly down river. Mim dipped her

toes in the cold water. "This is too slow!" Zak groaned.

He began to row the boat.

There were _ _ _ _ _ _ _

_ _ the _ _ _ _. Zak _ _ _

_ _ _ _ _ _ _ _ _ _ _ _ _.

They _ _ _ _ _ _

_ _ _ _ _ down the river.

_ _ _ dipped   her _ _ _ _

_ _ the _ _ _ _ water.

"This _ _ too _ _ _!" Zak

_ _ _ _ _ _.

He began to _ _ the _ _ _.

Copy the text from the top scroll to the bottom scroll. Write a sound on each line,
e.g. b oa t. Where the vowel spelling is split (o–e), there is a link, e.g. c o d e .
This activity can also be used for dictation.
This sheet may be photocopied by the purchaser. © Phonic Books Ltd 2014

Book 3:   New words

Explain these words:

current – _____   seep – _____

rapids – _____   probe – _____

shoal   – _____   ragged – _____

Link the sentences so that they make sense:

Rapids start where a	water began to seep in.
Mim wanted to jump into the	river becomes narrow.
At first, the shadow in the river	so that the catfish could not get him.
The boat hit the rocks and	river and float with the current.
The catfish probed the riverbed	because the otter had bitten it.
The catfish tail was ragged	looked like a shoal of fish.
The otter jumped onto the river bank	with its long whiskers.

Discuss the new words in the text and get the reader to explain them verbally and then in writing (the reader may need help with spelling). The reader can then match the two parts of the sentence.
This sheet may be photocopied by the purchaser. © Phonic Books Ltd 2014

Book 3: Comprehension 1

Shadow in the River – what's missing?

The boat tipped. Out jumped a massive catfish. It grabbed Zak by the elbow. Zak was dragged into the river below. The catfish monster tossed Zak to and fro. The talisman fell onto the riverbed. The long whiskers probed the riverbed. Oh no! The catfish was very close to the talisman.

Read the text above. Spot what is missing from the picture. Add it to the picture. For students who enjoy drawing, photocopy the text without the picture. Ask them to read the passage and draw a picture that fits the description. This sheet may be photocopied by the purchaser. © Phonic Books Ltd 2014

Book 3: Writing

The catfish – what is it like?

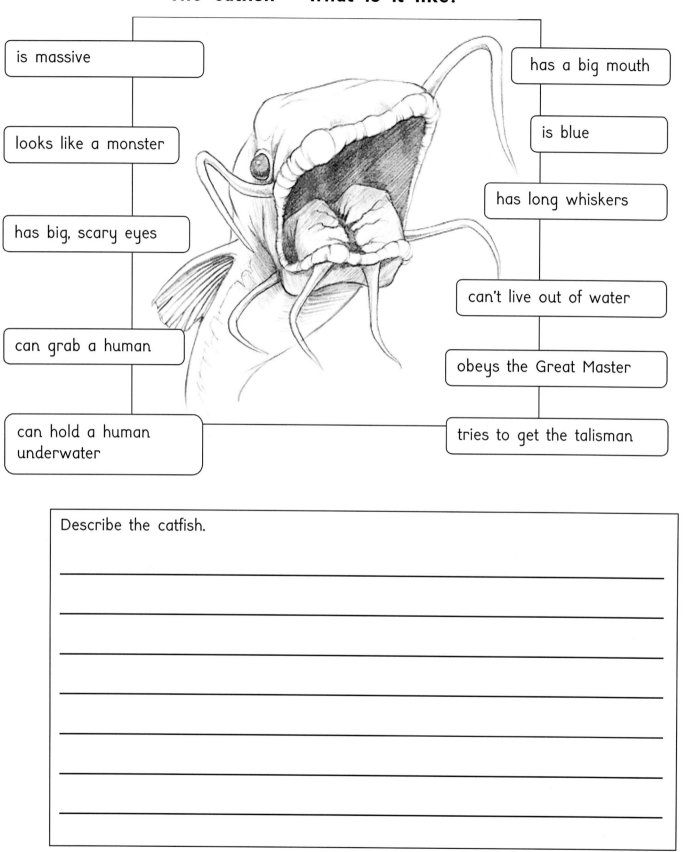

is massive

looks like a monster

has big, scary eyes

can grab a human

can hold a human underwater

has a big mouth

is blue

has long whiskers

can't live out of water

obeys the Great Master

tries to get the talisman

Describe the catfish.

Describe the catfish. You can use some of the words in the labels. This sheet may be photocopied by the purchaser. © Phonic Books Ltd 2014

Book 3: Comprehension 2

Catfish – true or false?

Catfish are called catfish because they have barbels which look like a cat's whiskers. There are more than 100 different kinds of catfish. They can be tiny and they can be massive. Some have scales. Others are covered in slime or body armor. Catfish live in fresh water, like lakes and rivers. They can be found all over the world. Some catfish like to live in caves underwater. Most catfish have a flat head, a big mouth and small eyes. They use their whiskers to find food. The biggest catfish ever caught was the Mekong catfish in Thailand. It was 10 feet long and weighed 650 pounds. Most catfish are not dangerous to humans.

Is it true?	yes	no
Catfish are a small group of fish.	☐	☐
Catfish can be lots of different sizes.	☐	☐
All catfish have scales.	☐	☐
Catfish like to live in the sea.	☐	☐
Catfish find food with their whiskers.	☐	☐
The biggest catfish ever caught was in Thailand.	☐	☐

Read the text. Now read the sentences below and put a check in the boxes according to whether they are true or false. This sheet may be photocopied by the purchaser.

Book 3: Splitting two-syllable words with 'oe' spellings

open		o	pen		<u>open</u>
hopeless					_____
moaning					_____
narrow					_____
woeful					_____
joking					_____
lonely					_____
boastful					_____
tiptoe					_____
borrow					_____
hero					_____
homeless					_____
oboe					_____

This activity allows the student to practice splitting two-syllable words. The teacher can use his/her own approach to splitting syllables (see page 3 for the different approaches to splitting words into syllables). These words can be used for dictation. This sheet may be photocopied by the purchaser.

Book 3: Homophones 1: Which is which?

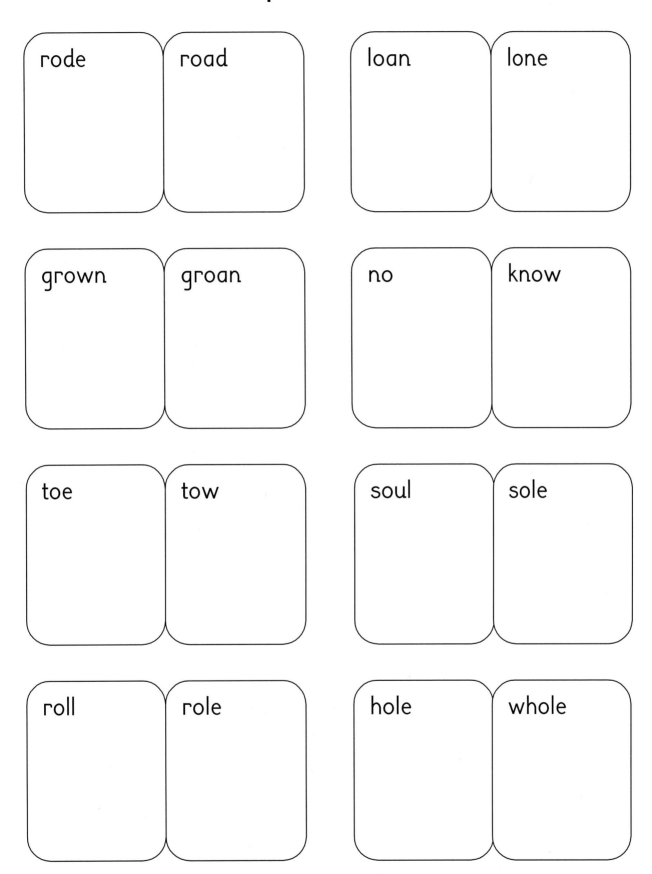

rode	road		loan	lone

grown	groan		no	know

toe	tow		soul	sole

roll	role		hole	whole

The student can draw an image on each card to help him/her remember the meaning of the word.
Photocopy the cards and play 'Concentration'. Spread the cards face down and players take turns to
find matching homophone pairs. This sheet may be photocopied by the purchaser.

48

Book 3: Homophones 2: Toe or tow?

1. A _____ truck took away the car when it broke down.

2. I stubbed my _____ on a stone.

3. I _____ my bike to school.

4. There was a traffic jam on the main _____.

5. I ate the _____ bag of potato chips.

6. There is a _____ in my bag.

7. Jack has _____ 2 inches in the last year.

8. The kids _____ when they do their homework.

9. I love _____ music.

10. The bubble gum stuck to the _____ of my shoe.

11. I don't _____ what I will be when I grow up.

12. "_____! You can't go to the movies tonight."

13. I would like to play the _____ of the bad guy.

14. It's your turn to _____ the dice.

15. Dad went to the bank to get a _____.

16. The _____ wolf went to hunt in the hills.

| soul sole | rode road | whole hole | lone loan |
| toe tow | no know | roll role | grown groan |

Read the sentences above. The student can use the homophone cards from the previous page to select the correct homophone for each sentence. This sheet may be photocopied by the purchaser. © Phonic Books Ltd 2014

Book 3: Stepping stones game: 'oe'

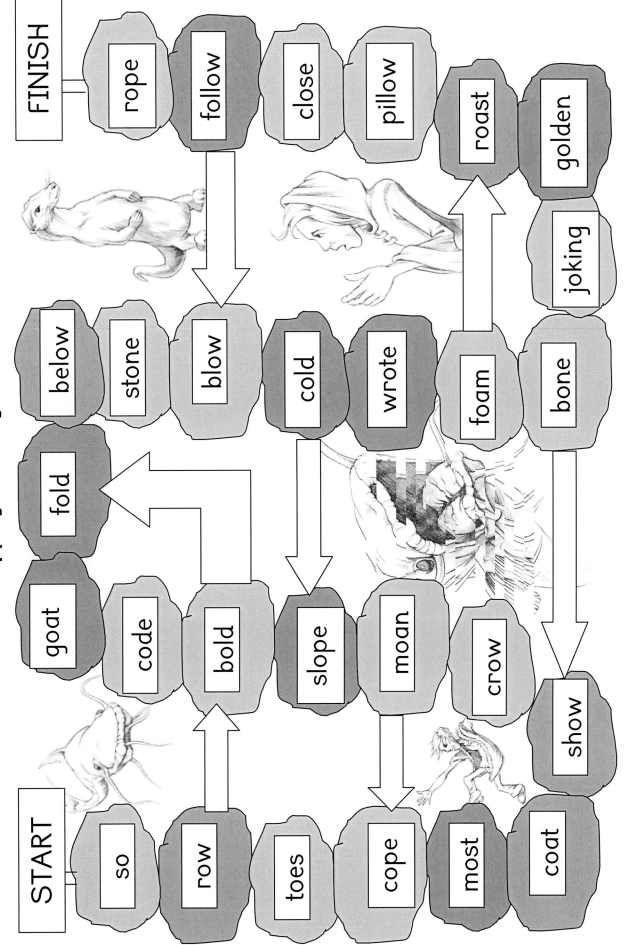

FINISH

rope

follow

close

pillow

roast

golden

joking

below

stone

blow

cold

wrote

foam

bone

fold

goat

code

bold

slope

moan

crow

show

START

so

row

toes

cope

most

coat

Book 3: 4-in-a-row game: 'oe'

glow	foe	load	bold	no
elbow	roast	soap	mole	snow
moat	sold	tone	joke	goes
slope	blown	grope	bloat	zero
throw	shoal	goal	hole	post
foal	cone	show	token	woe
vote	hoe	know	toast	ghost

Play with two sets of colored counters. Two players take turns to read the word and put a counter on the word. The winner is the first to get four of his or her counters in a row. The winner places a counter on a talisman. The game is played four times until all the talismans are covered. This sheet may be photocopied by the purchaser. © Phonic Books Ltd 2014

Book 4: Deep Sea Danger

Questions for discussion

Chapter 1

1. What time of day is 'first light'? (p. 1)

2. Why does the author use the words 'curled and twirled' to describe the seaweed in the sea? (p. 3)

Chapter 2

1. How does Mim react when she sees the way Zak is opening the clams? (p. 7)

2. What was Zak thinking about when they found the pearl? (p. 8)

Chapter 3

1. When Mim gets stung, it says she 'nurses her leg'. What does that mean? (p. 10)

2. What was lurking under the boat? (p. 11)

Chapter 4

1. Why do you think Zak turned into a turtle? (p. 14)

2. How does the story end? (p. 16)

Book 4: Blending and segmenting: er, ir, ur, or, ear

fur	f	ur		
sir				
term				
word				
earn				
church				
twirl				
nerve				
worth				
learn				
burst				
flirt				
world				

Blend the sounds into a word. Segment the word into sounds by writing one sound in each square. Segmenting words into sounds may vary according to regional pronunciation. This sheet may be photocopied by the purchaser. © Phonic Books Ltd 2014

Book 4: Reading and sorting words with er, ir, ur, or, ear

er	ur	ir	or	ear

her	first	burp	worm
world	earn	purse	jerk
early	bird	serve	turn
worth	heard	curl	curb
dirty	verse	work	learn
curse	worse	birth	whirl
murder	sister	stir	expert
search	worship	disturb	further

Photocopy this page onto card and cut out the words. Read and sort the cards out according to the 'er' headings at the top of the page. This sheet may be photocopied by the purchaser.
© Phonic Books Ltd. 2009.

54

Book 4: Spellings: er, ir, ur, or, ear

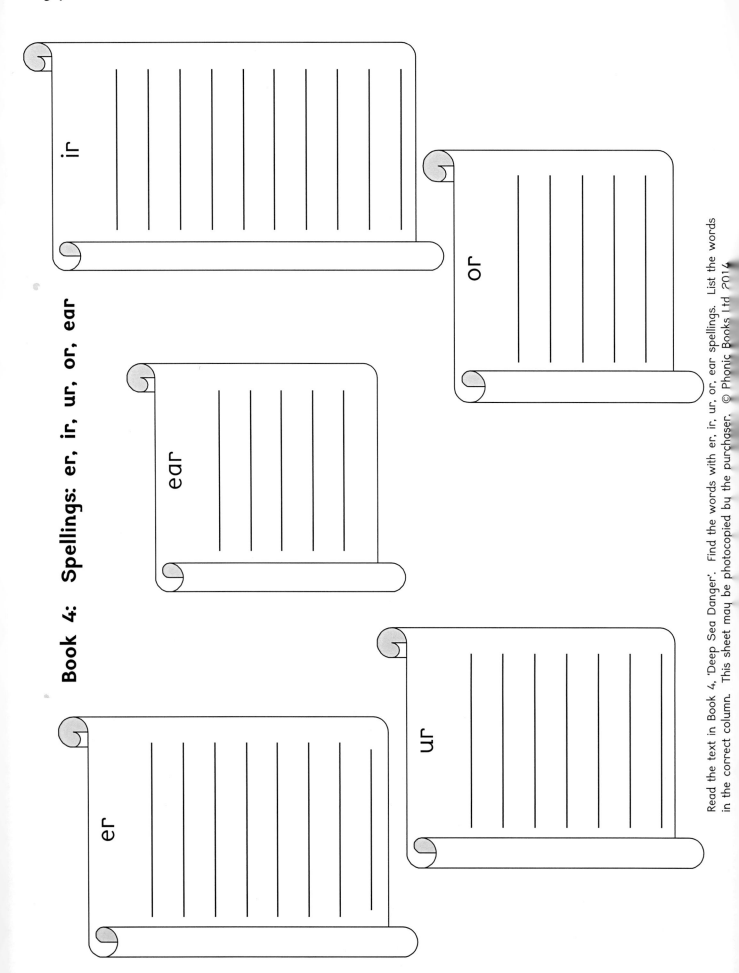

ir

or

ear

er

ur

Read the text in Book 4, 'Deep Sea Danger'. Find the words with er, ir, ur, or, or ear spellings. List the words in the correct column. This sheet may be photocopied by the purchaser. © Phonic Books Ltd 2014

Book 4: Reading and spelling

Mim did not want to disturb Zak. She slipped into the water. She searched for clams on the seabed. The seaweed curled and twirled around her. "This water world is so cool," she said to herself.

<u>M</u> <u>i</u> <u>m</u> _ _ _   _ _ _   want to

_ _ _ _ _ _   Zak.   She

_ _ _ _ _ _   into the _ _ _ _.

She   _ _ _ _ _   for

_ _ _ _ _ _ _   the seabed.

The   seaweed _ _ _ _ _   and

_ _ _ _ _ _   around _ _.

"This _ _ _ _ _   _ _ _ _ _ is so

cool!" she said to _ _ _ _ _ _ _.

Copy the text in the top scroll to the bottom scroll. Write a sound on each line, e.g. <u>b</u> <u>ur</u> <u>n</u>. This activity can also be used for dictation. This sheet may be photocopied by the purchaser. © Phonic Books Ltd 2014

Book 4: New words

Explain these words:

twirled – _____   hurl –   _____

surface – _____   whimper – _____

stern –   _____   drifted – _____

Link the sentences so that they make sense:

The seaweed twirled and	in a stern voice.
After Mim had the clams,	curled around Mim.
When Zak cut his finger,	under the boat.
Zak hurled himself	she swam up to the surface.
Mim spoke to Zak	into the sea.
The boat drifted	he whimpered.
The jellyfish was lurking	along the river.

Book 4:   Comprehension 1

The pearl – what's missing?

At first, Zak held the pearl up. Then he turned it round and round. It was perfect. It was the most perfect pearl in the world. "This pearl could be worth something. We could earn a lot of money," he murmured. He began to think about how much the pearl could be worth.

Read the text above. Spot what is missing from the picture. Add it to the picture. For students who enjoy drawing, photocopy the text without the picture. Ask them to read the passage and draw a picture that fits the description. This sheet may be photocopied by the purchaser. © Phonic Books Ltd 2014

Book 4: Writing

The jellyfish – what is it like?

is massive

is green, blue and transparent

has very long stingers

uses the stingers to find food

has no bones

has no brain, heart or blood

propels itself by shooting water from its mouth

can be found all over the world

this jellyfish is not deadly, but some jellyfish are

Describe the jellyfish.

_____
_____
_____
_____
_____
_____
_____

Describe the jellyfish. You can use some of the words in the labels. This sheet may be photocopied by the purchaser. © Phonic Books Ltd 2014

Book 4: Comprehension 2

Jellyfish – true or false?

Did you know that jellyfish are really odd animals? They have no brain, no heart and no bones. Jellyfish have been around for 650 million years. They are older than dinosaurs and sharks. Jellyfish have tentacles with stingers on them, to catch their prey. Mostly, they eat small fish and plankton (tiny sea animals and plants). Jellyfish move by shooting water which propels them in the water. The world's biggest jellyfish is 8 feet wide. The tentacles are as long as half a football field. Most jellyfish are not dangerous to humans but some are. The box jellyfish can kill a human in three minutes. Did you know some people like to eat jellyfish?

Is it true?	yes	no
Jellyfish have no brain, no heart and no bones.	☐	☐
Dinosaurs are older than jellyfish.	☐	☐
Jellyfish use their tentacles and stingers to catch food.	☐	☐
Jellyfish use their tentacles to swim.	☐	☐
All jellyfish can kill humans.	☐	☐
Some jellyfish like to eat humans.	☐	☐

Read the text. Now read the sentences below and put a check in the boxes according to whether they are true or false. This sheet may be photocopied by the purchaser.

60

Book 4: Splitting two-syllable words with er, ir, ur, or, ear spellings

thirteen	thir	teen	thirteen
murder			_____
person			_____
earning			_____
worship			_____
thirsty			_____
disturb			_____
expert			_____
early			_____
worker			_____
birthday			_____
further			_____
permit			_____

This activity allows the student to practice splitting two-syllable words. The teacher can use his/her own approach to splitting syllables (see page 3 for the different approaches to splitting words into syllables). These words can be used for dictation. This sheet may be photocopied by the purchaser.

© Phonic Books Ltd 2014

Book 4:   Homophones 1: Which is which?

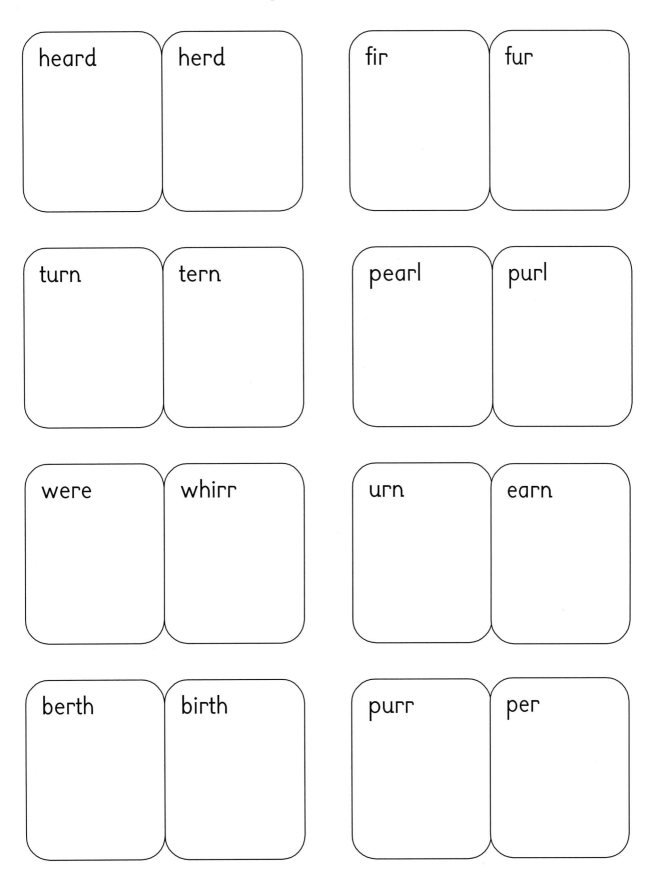

heard	herd		fir	fur
pearl	purl		turn	tern
were	whirr		urn	earn
berth	birth		purr	per

The student can draw an image on each card to help him/her remember the meaning of the word.
Photocopy the cards and play 'Concentration'. Spread the cards face down and players take turns to
find matching homophone pairs. This sheet may be photocopied by the purchaser.

1.   The man planted a _____ tree.

2.   Rabbits have very soft _____.

3.   I _____ the gossip at school.

4.   The farmer had a _____ of cows.

5.   We _____ waiting by the bus stop.

6.   Dad turned on the fan and it began to _____.

7.   _____ to the left and you will see the school.

8.   The _____ is an amazing bird.

9.   My cat gave _____ to six little kittens.

10.   On the ferry, I slept on a wooden _____.

11.   The cat sat by the fire and began to _____.

12.   The cost is $5.00 _____ book.

13.   Jack went to fill up the _____ with hot water.

14.   When I start the job, I will _____ $100 a week.

15.   The _____ necklace was a gift from her grandpa.

16.   _____ is a knitting stitch.

fir fur	turn tern	were whirr	pearl purl
purr per	berth birth	urn earn	heard herd

Read the sentences above. The student can use the homophone cards from the previous page to select the correct homophone for each sentence. This sheet may be photocopied by the purchaser. © Phonic Books Ltd 2014

Book 4: Stepping stones game: er, ir, ur, or, ear

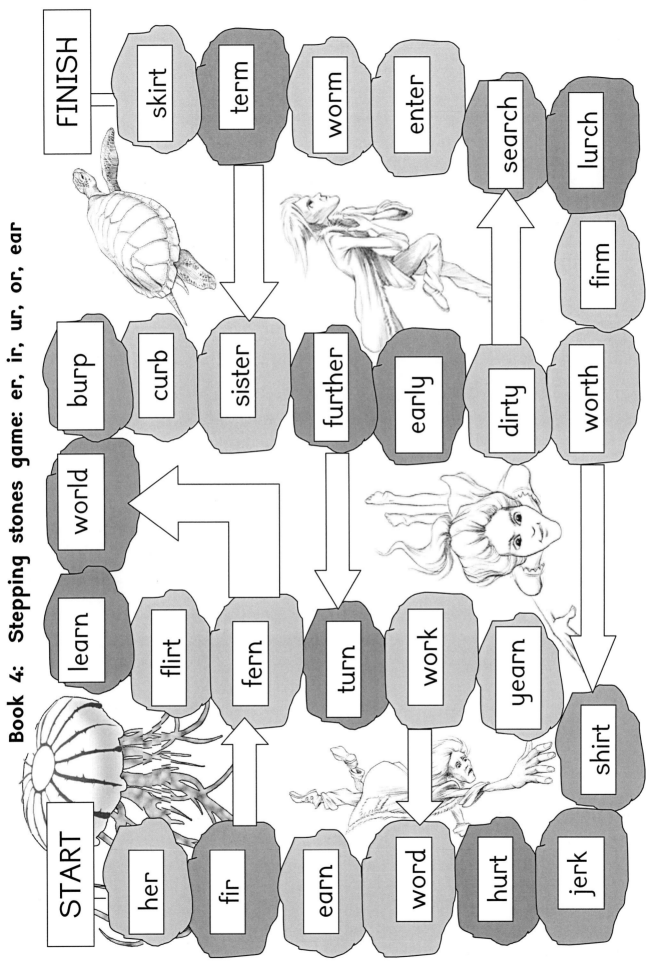

START
her
fir
earn
word
hurt
jerk
shirt
yearn
work
turn
fern
flirt
learn
world
burp
curb
sister
further
early
dirty
worth
firm
lurch
search
enter
worm
term
skirt
FINISH

Book 4: 4-in-a-row game: er, ir, ur, or, ear

dirt	urn	learn	worse	perk
burp	worm	firm	germ	first
jerk	earn	verse	stir	fur
birth	worth	heard	burn	curb
early	curl	whirl	dirty	world
girl	father	motor	lurk	after
over	work	shirt	fir	turn

Play with two sets of colored counters. Two players take turns to read the word and put a counter on the word. The winner is the first to get four of his or her counters in a row. The winner places a counter on a talisman. The game is played four times until all the talismans are covered. This sheet may be photocopied by the purchaser. © Phonic Books Ltd 2014

Book 5: Hounded in the Snow

Questions for discussion

Chapter 1

   1. In what kind of landscape is the story set? (p. 1)

   2. Why you think Zak's spirits sank? (p. 2)

Chapter 2

   1. What did Mim trip over? (p. 6)

   2. Mim wanted to turn back, but she didn't. Why? (p. 7)

Chapter 3

   1. When Mim and Zak sit in the snow cave, they hear howling.

      What do you think they were thinking? (p. 9)

Chapter 4

   1. Zak and Mim see footprints again. What do they realize?

      (p. 10)

   2. Zak says, "I'll be a decoy!" What does he mean? (p. 12)

Chapter 5

   1. The story is called 'Hounded in the Snow'. Do you think that

      is a good title for it? Why? (p. 16)

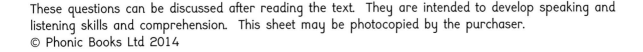

Book 5: Blending and segmenting: 'ow'

word					
out	ou	t			
how					
loud					
town					
pouch					
brown					
sound					
drown					
mouth					
scowl					
ground					
howling					
about					

Blend the sounds into a word. Segment the word into sounds by writing one sound in each square.
This sheet may be photocopied by the purchaser. © Phonic Books Ltd 2014

Book 5:   Blending and segmenting: 'oi'

toy	t	oy			
oil					
boy					
coin					
soya					
voice					
enjoy					
spoil					
loyal					
avoid					
ahoy					
toilet					
employ					

Blend the sounds into a word. Segment the word into sounds by writing one sound in each square.
This sheet may be photocopied by the purchaser. © Phonic Books Ltd 2014

Book 5: Reading and sorting words
with 'ow' and 'oi' spellings

ow	ou

ouch	power	shout	frown
howl	round	aloud	towel
allow	spout	shower	bound

oi	oy

soil	toy	royal	voice
boy	enjoy	point	toilet
annoy	coin	destroy	spoilt

Book 5:   Spelling: 'ow' and 'oi'

ow

ou

oi

oy

Read the text in Book 5, 'Hounded in the Snow'. Find the words with 'ow' and 'oi' spellings.
List the words in the correct column. This sheet may be photocopied by the purchaser.

Book 5: Reading and spelling

Mim pointed to the tracks in the snow. She frowned.

"Look! Footprints! Our footprints!" she called out loud.

"We're going round and round!" She was getting

very annoyed. Just then, the kids heard a loud growl.

M i m _ _ _ _ _ _ _ to the

_ _ _ _ _ in the snow. She

_ _ _ _ _ _. "Look! Footprints!

_ _ _ _ _ _ _ _ _ _ _ _ _ !"

she called _ _ _ _ _ _. "We're

going _ _ _ _ and _ _ _ _ !"

She was getting _ _ _ _ annoyed.

_ _ _ _ then, the _ _ _ _ heard

a _ _ _ _ _ _ _ _ _.

Copy the text from the top scroll to the bottom scroll. Write a sound on each line,
e.g. h ow l. This activity can also be used for dictation.

Book 5: New words

Explain these words:

shrouded – _____   scowled – _____

vowed – _____   bounded – _____

decoy – _____   trudge – _____

Link the sentences so that they make sense:

To trudge is to walk	anger.
Mim vowed she would be	slowly and heavily.
Zak was a decoy so	the distance.
The Yeti scowled in	that the Yeti would not attack Mim.
The stag bounded off into	fell to the ground.
The ice caps were shrouded in	as brave as any boy.
Mim tripped on the skull and	a thick mist.

Book 5:   Comprehension 1

The Yeti – what's missing?

Out of the mist loomed the giant Yeti. It towered over Zak. It had long fur and big, powerful hands. The hands had long nails. The Yeti had pointed ears and a big, black mouth. He made terrible growling sounds. Zak was just a boy. How was he going to fight him? Zak grabbed hold of the talisman.

Read the text above. Spot what is missing from the picture. Add it to the picture. For students who enjoy drawing, photocopy the text without the picture. Ask them to read the passage and draw a picture that fits the description. This sheet may be photocopied by the purchaser. © Phonic Books Ltd 2014

Book 5: Writing

The Yeti – what is it like?

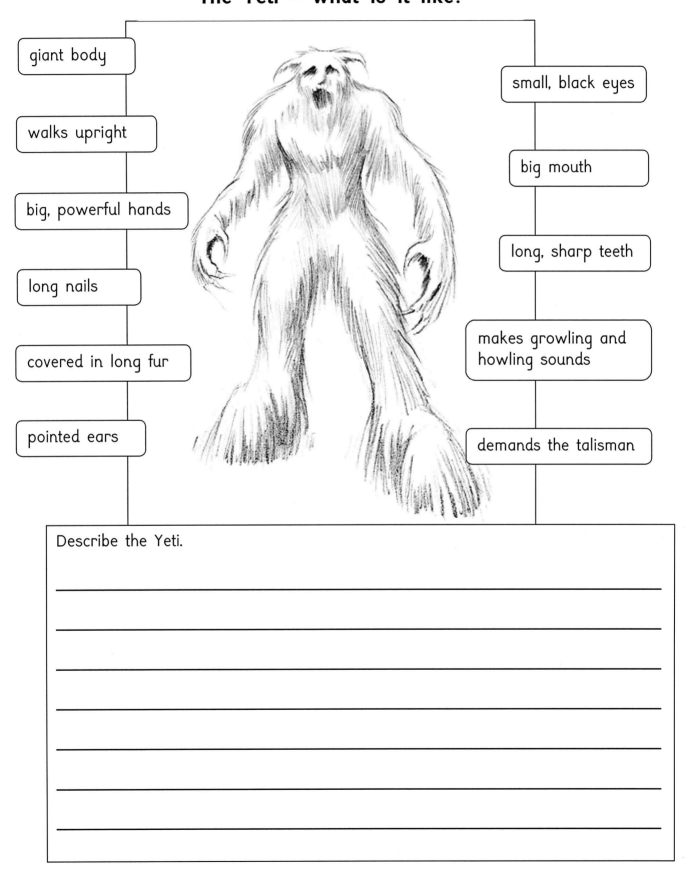

giant body

walks upright

big, powerful hands

long nails

covered in long fur

pointed ears

small, black eyes

big mouth

long, sharp teeth

makes growling and howling sounds

demands the talisman

Describe the Yeti.

_____

_____

_____

_____

_____

_____

Describe the Yeti. You can use some of the words in the labels. This sheet may be photocopied by the purchaser. © Phonic Books Ltd 2014

Book 5: Comprehension 2

The Yeti – true or false?

The Yeti is a giant creature which, some people claim, lives in the Himalayan Mountains in Nepal. It is ape–like and walks upright. It is also called the Abominable Snowman. It is part of the local legends. Many people have said that they have spotted a giant animal like the Yeti, but it has never been proven. Scientists believe that the Yeti is just a legend, like Bigfoot in North America and the Loch Ness Monster in Scotland. People have found giant footprints in the snow, but there are other possible explanations: bears, other apes or a human hermit. Many books and films have been made about the Yeti.

Is it true?	yes	no
The Yeti is said to live in the sea.	☐	☐
The Yeti is said to walk upright.	☐	☐
Many people claim to have seen the Yeti.	☐	☐
They have found giant footprints.	☐	☐
The Yeti is a real animal.	☐	☐
The footprints could belong to a bear, ape or human.	☐	☐

Read the text. Now read the sentences below and put a check in the boxes according to whether they are true or false. This sheet may be photocopied by the purchaser.

Book 5: Splitting two-syllable words with 'ow' spellings

power	pow	er	<u>power</u>
loudest			_____
pouting			_____
drowsy			_____
voucher			_____
outing			_____
grounded			_____
towel			_____
bouncy			_____
howling			_____
mouthful			_____
flower			_____
rebound			_____

This activity allows the student to practice splitting two-syllable words. The teacher can use his/her own approach to splitting syllables (see page 3 for the different approaches to splitting words into syllables). These words can be used for dictation. This sheet may be photocopied by the purchaser.
© Phonic Books Ltd 2014

Book 5: Splitting two-syllable words with 'oi' spellings

Word	Syllable 1	Syllable 2	Write
enjoy	en	joy	<u>enjoy</u>
convoy			_____
poison			_____
employ			_____
toilet			_____
destroy			_____
avoid			_____
decoy			_____
noisy			_____
annoy			_____
boiling			_____
royal			_____
ointment			_____

This activity allows the student to practice splitting two-syllable words. The teacher can use his/her own approach to splitting syllables (see page 3 for the different approaches to splitting words into syllables). These words can be used for dictation. This sheet may be photocopied by the purchaser.

Book 5: Stepping stones game: 'ow' and 'oi'

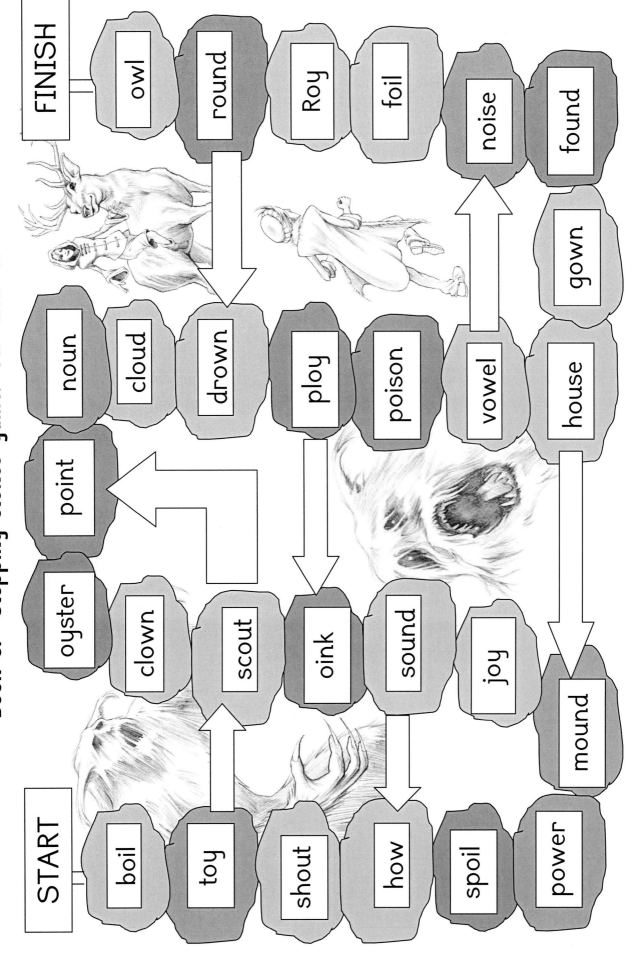

FINISH

owl

round

Roy

foil

noise

found

noun

cloud

drown

ploy

poison

vowel

gown

point

house

oyster

clown

scout

oink

sound

joy

mound

START

boil

toy

shout

how

spoil

power

This game is for 1–4 players. Play with counters and die. This sheet may be photocopied by the purchaser. © Phonic Books Ltd 2014

77

Book 5: 4-in-a-row game: 'ow' and 'oi'

loud	toil	fowl	round	toy
noise	out	town	pout	house
spoil	boy	boil	mount	allow
voice	Roy	proud	howl	coin
poise	annoy	crowd	coil	point
joint	ploy	how	sound	noun
toilet	royal	spout	frown	brow

Play with two sets of colored counters. Two players take turns to read the word and put a counter on the word. The winner is the first to get four of his or her counters in a row. The winner places a counter on a talisman. The game is played four times until all the talismans are covered. This sheet may be photocopied by the purchaser. © Phonic Books Ltd 2014

Book 5: Reading and sorting words with <ow> spelling

snow	**c**ow

now	blow	tow	low
howl	growl	mow	bow
flow	know	crown	crow
allow	glow	brow	town
slow	show	brown	fowl
jowl	power	bowl	row
vow	throw	trowel	towel
sow	shower	yellow	flower

Book 6: Death at Noon

Questions for discussion

Chapter 1

1. What time of day is noon? (p. 1)

2. Why is Mim in a bad mood? (p. 2)

Chapter 2

1. How do Mim and Zak find a drink? (p. 4)

2. Mim warns Zak about camels. What does she say? (p. 6)

Chapter 3

1. Why is Zak sitting in the sand, looking foolish? (p. 8)

2. What does the word 'scrub' mean in this story? (p. 9)

Chapter 4

1. What does the dragon snake look like? (pp. 10, 11)

Chapter 5

1. How does the dragon snake control Zak and Mim? (p. 12)

2. How does Mim 'save the day'? (pp. 13, 14)

3. Why do you think Zak turned into a mongoose? (p. 15)

Book 6: Blending and segmenting: 'oo'

too	t	oo
you		
rude		u		e
chew		
truth				
clue			
boot			
soup			
rule				
threw			
July				
cruel				
flute				

Blend the sounds into a word. Segment the word into sounds by writing one sound in each square. Split vowel spellings (u–e) are represented by half squares linked together. This sheet may be photocopied by the purchaser. © Phonic Books Ltd 2014

Book 6: Reading and sorting words with 'oo' spellings

oo	ou	ue	u-e	ew	u

pool	rude	blue	group
grew	July	shoot	youth
flew	rule	true	brutal
glue	scoop	crude	chew
route	judo	smooth	sue
brute	jewel	include	gruesome
shampoo	scuba	coupon	plume
drew	proof	loose	crew

Book 6: Spelling: 'oo'

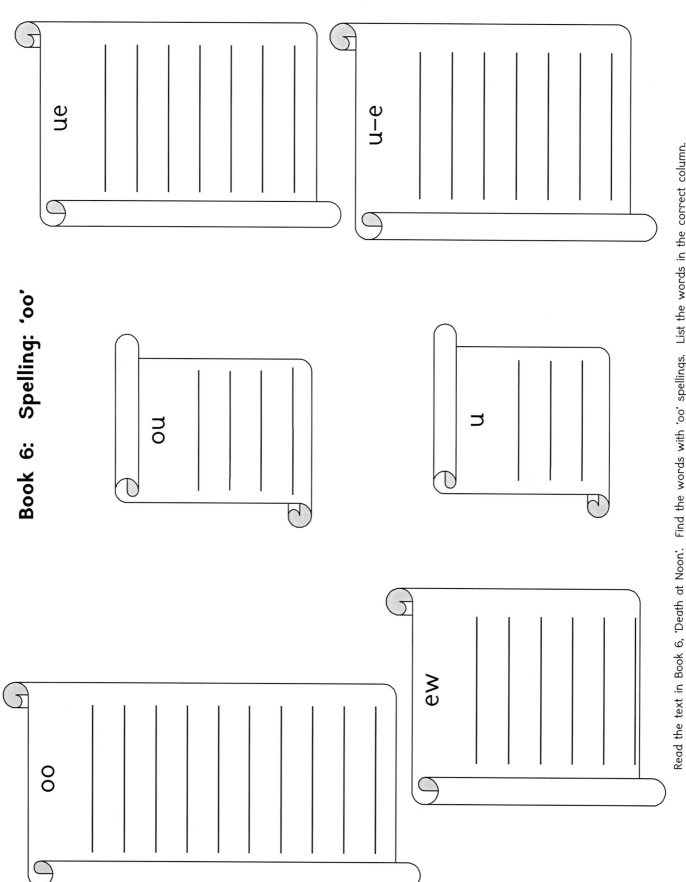

oo

ou

ue

u–e

u

ew

Read the text in Book 6, 'Death at Noon'. Find the words with 'oo' spellings. List the words in the correct column.

Book 6: Reading and spelling

The snake flew out of the scrub.   It loomed over Zak.

It glared at him with its cruel eyes. The snake began

to sway. "I will rule over you," it seemed to say.

Zak and Mim fell under its spell. They were doomed.

The   snake _ _ __   out of the

_ _ _ _ _.   It   _ __ _ __   over

_ _ _.   It glared _ _ _ _ _

_ _ __   its   _ _ __ _   eyes.

The _ _ _ _ _ began to _ _ __.

"I   _ _ __   _ _ _ _   over

_ __,"   it seemed to say.   _ _ _

and _ _ _   _ _ __   under its

_ _ _ __.   They were   _ __ _ __.

Book 6: New words

Explain these words:

gloomily – _____   brute – _____

gruesome – _____   frantic – _____

conclude – _____   loomed – _____

Link the sentences so that they make sense:

"We have no drink and no food,"	camels were brutes.
The dragon snake had such cruel eyes,	Mim said gloomily.
Mim warned Zak that	over Zak, he could see its fangs.
"The truth is, you never listen,"	it was gruesome.
Mim was frantic and she	in the scrub.
When the dragon snake loomed	didn't know what to do.
The dragon snake was hiding	Mim concluded.

Discuss the new words in the text and get the reader to explain them verbally and then in writing (the reader may need help with spelling). The reader can then match the two parts of the sentence.
This sheet may be photocopied by the purchaser. © Phonic Books Ltd 2014

Book 6: Comprehension 1

The dragon snake – what's missing?

The dragon snake loomed over Zak and Mim. It had smooth, slimy skin. It had cruel eyes that seemed to say, "I will rule over you." Zak could see the long fangs dripping with venom. The dragon drew closer. It began to sway.   Soon Zak and Mim were swaying too.

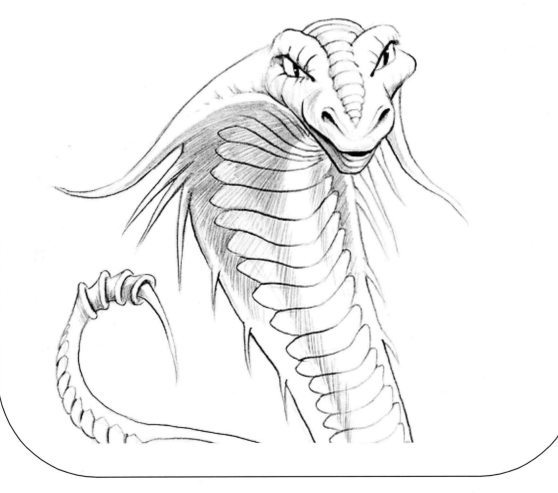

Read the text above. Spot what is missing from the picture. Add it to the picture. For students who enjoy drawing, photocopy the text without the picture. Ask them to read the passage and draw a picture that fits the description. This sheet may be photocopied by the purchaser. © Phonic Books Ltd 2014

88

Book 6: Writing

The dragon snake – what is it like?

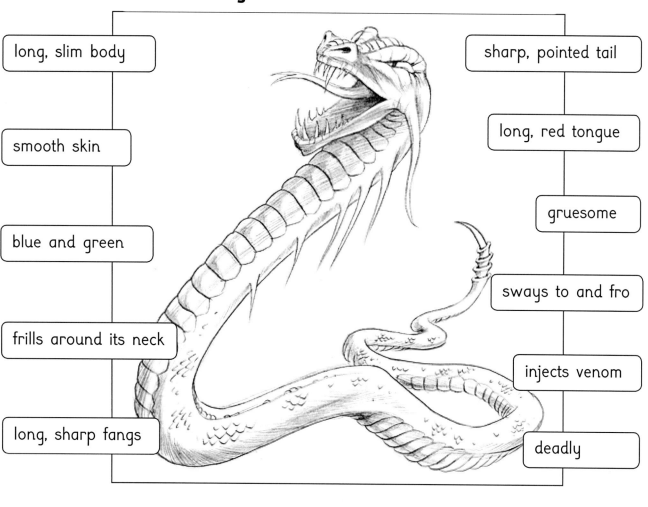

long, slim body

smooth skin

blue and green

frills around its neck

long, sharp fangs

sharp, pointed tail

long, red tongue

gruesome

sways to and fro

injects venom

deadly

Describe the dragon snake.

_____

_____

_____

_____

_____

_____

_____

Describe the dragon snake. You can use some of the words in the labels. This sheet may be photocopied by the purchaser. © Phonic Books Ltd 2014

Book 6: Comprehension 2

Mongooses – true or false?

The mongoose is a mammal that lives in South Asia, Africa and South Europe. There are 30 different kinds of mongooses. Some are as small as squirrels; others are as big as cats. Some kinds of mongooses live and hunt on their own; others live and hunt in groups. Mongooses are carnivores. They eat insects, crabs, lizards, snakes, chickens, eggs and dead animals. They are very quick and cunning. The Indian mongoose is used to fight and kill venomous snakes. Mongooses are clever and can learn tricks. Some people keep them as pets to kill rats.

Is it true?	yes	no
Mongooses are squirrels.	☐	☐
There are 30 different kinds of mongoose.	☐	☐
They live in big groups.	☐	☐
Mongooses like to eat meat.	☐	☐
Indian mongooses are kept to fight and kill snakes.	☐	☐
Mongooses can learn tricks because they are cute.	☐	☐

Read the text. Now read the sentences below and put a check in the boxes according to whether they are true or false. This sheet may be photocopied by the purchaser.
© Phonic Books Ltd 2014

Book 6: Splitting two-syllable words with 'oo' spellings

bamboo	bam	boo	bamboo
youthful			_____
chewing			_____
truthful			_____
clueless			_____
include			_____
scooter			_____
coupon			_____
Andrew			_____
brutal			_____
gruesome			_____
intrude			_____
tattoo			_____

This activity allows the student to practice splitting two-syllable words. The teacher can use his/her own approach to splitting syllables (see page 3 for the different approaches to splitting words into syllables). These words can be used for dictation. This sheet may be photocopied by the purchaser.

Book 6: Homophones 1: Which is which?

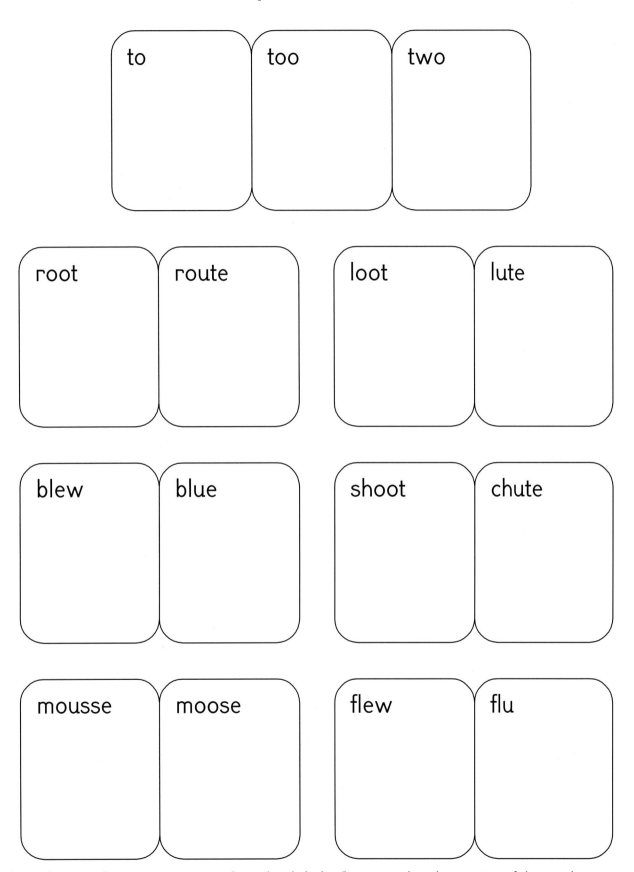

| to | too | two |

| root | route |

| loot | lute |

| blew | blue |

| shoot | chute |

| mousse | moose |

| flew | flu |

The student can draw an image on each card to help him/her remember the meaning of the word. Photocopy the cards and play 'Concentration'. Spread the cards face down and players take turns to find matching homophone pairs. With the words to, too, two the players will need to find all three cards. This sheet may be photocopied by the purchaser. © Phonic Books Ltd 2014

Book 6: Homophones 2: Blue or blew?

1. The flag was red, white and _____.

2. The wind _____ the clouds across the sky.

3. I went _____ the store with my Mom.

4. The cat had three black and _____ white kittens.

5. "I want ice cream _____!" yelled the little boy.

6. I love chocolate _____.

7. A _____ is a big kind of deer.

8. A carrot is the _____ of the plant.

9. We took the shortest _____ home.

10. The burglar put the _____ in a sack.

11. A _____ is a very old instrument.

12. The hunter tried to _____ the deer.

13. There is a water _____ in the swimming pool.

14. On Sunday, we _____ by plane to New York.

15. My dad is sick with the _____.

| blew blue | root route | shoot chute | flew flu |

| mousse moose | to too two | loot lute |

Read the sentences above. The student can use the homophone cards from the previous page to select the correct homophone for each sentence. This sheet may be photocopied by the purchaser. © Phonic Books Ltd 2014

Book 6: Stepping stones game: 'oo'

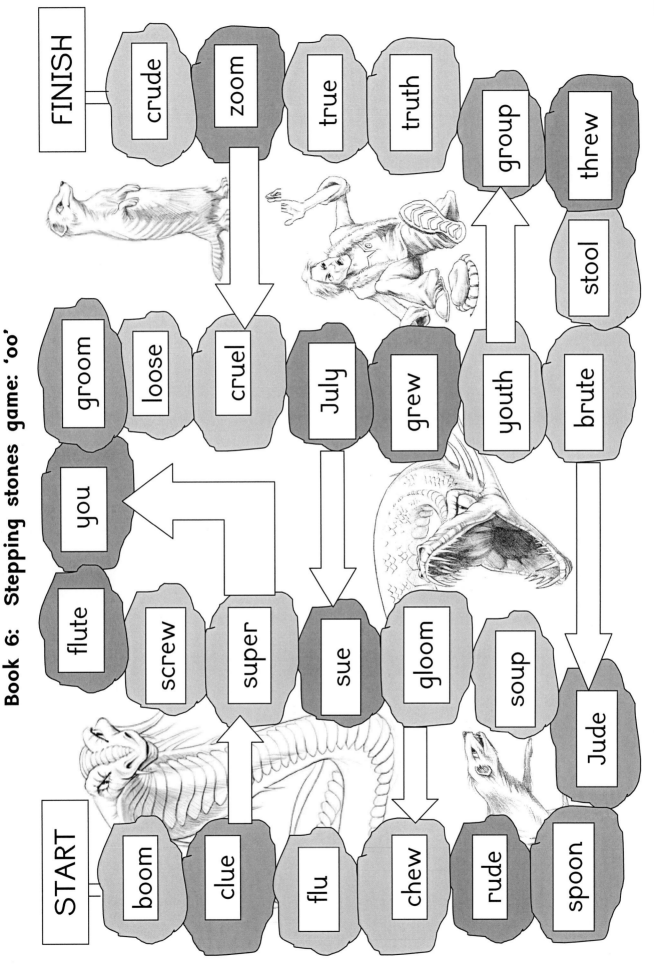

FINISH

crude

zoom

true

truth

group

threw

stool

groom

loose

cruel

July

grew

youth

brute

you

flute

screw

super

sue

gloom

soup

Jude

START

boom

clue

flu

chew

rude

spoon

Book 6: 4-in-a-row game: 'oo'

you	blew	loot	boom	clue
drew	rude	flu	flute	brew
true	stoop	lute	noon	super
soup	blue	rule	route	loose
group	brutal	jewel	cruel	June
gloom	sue	grew	judo	prune
glue	threw	truth	crude	loop

Play with two sets of colored counters. Two players take turns to read the word and put a counter on the word. The winner is the first to get four of his or her counters in a row. The winner places a counter on a talisman. The game is played four times until all the talismans are covered. This sheet may be photocopied by the purchaser. © Phonic Books Ltd 2014

Book 6: Reading and sorting words with <oo> spelling

look	pool

cook	fool	scoop	hook
food	hood	tool	drool
school	mood	good	wood
moon	spoon	ooze	took
room	crook	groom	stool
wool	root	foot	gloom
noon	shook	boot	brook
cool	balloon	woof	stood

Book 7: A Cry in the Dark

Questions for discussion

Chapter 1

1. Why did Zak get a tight feeling in his chest? (p. 2)

2. What did Mim step on in the cave? (p. 4)

Chapter 2

1. What do you think made the hairs on Zak's neck stand up?

   (p. 5)

2. What was the slimy thing gliding by? (p. 7)

Chapter 3

1. What did Mim run into? (p. 9)

Chapter 4

1. Why couldn't Mim get out of the web? (p. 11)

Chapter 5

1. Why couldn't the spider bite the scorpion? (p. 14)

2. How does the scorpion defeat the spider? (p. 14)

3. How does the scorpion set Mim free? (p. 15)

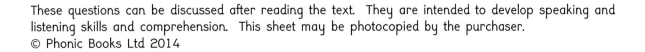

These questions can be discussed after reading the text. They are intended to develop speaking and listening skills and comprehension. This sheet may be photocopied by the purchaser.
© Phonic Books Ltd 2014

Book 7: Blending and segmenting: 'ie'

light	l	igh	t

tie

fine

by

mind

bright

drive

China

fries

shine

tonight

slimy

tried

Blend the sounds into a word. Segment the word into sounds by writing one sound in each square. Split vowel spellings (i–e) are represented by half squares linked together. This sheet may be photocopied by the purchaser. © Phonic Books Ltd 2014

Book 7: Reading and sorting words with 'ie' spellings

igh	ie	i-e	i	y

final	try	mine	high
life	dried	kite	slight
find	line	why	die
kind	dive	spies	nice
bright	lying	behind	fright
knife	shine	mile	style
giant	idol	midnight	flies
shy	thigh	slime	invite

Photocopy this page onto card and cut out the words. Read and sort the cards out according to the 'ie' headings at the top of the page. This sheet may be photocopied by the purchaser. © Phonic Books Ltd 2014

Book 7: Spelling: 'ie'

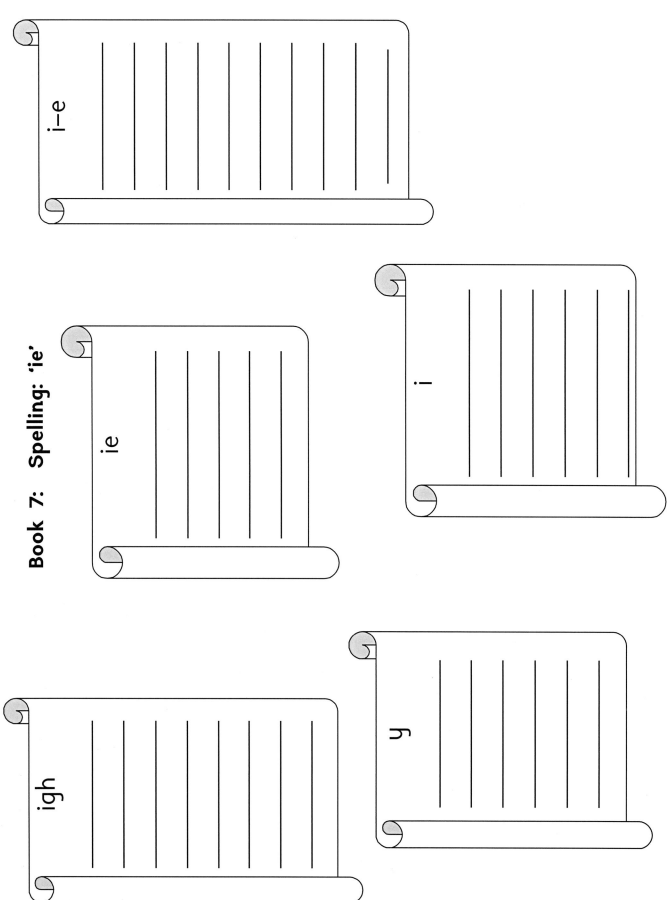

i–e

ie

igh

i

y

Read the text in Book 7, 'A Cry in the Dark'. Find the words with 'ie' spellings. List the words in the correct column.
This sheet may be photocopied by the purchaser. © Phonic Books Ltd 2014

Zak did not like caves. The cave was as black as night. Now he felt a tight feeling in his chest. He tried to think of the times the talisman had saved his life. Just then, something slimy came gliding by.

Z a k _ _ _   _ _ _

_ _ _ _   caves.   The cave was as

_ _ _ _   as   _ _ _ _.   Now

he   _ _ _ _   a   _ _ _ _   feeling

_ _   his   _ _ _ _.   He

_ _ _ _ _   to   _ _ _ _   of the

_ _ _ _ _   the talisman   _ _ _

saved   _ _ _   _ _ _ _.

_ _ _ _   then, something

_ _ _ _ _   came   _ _ _ _ _ _

_ _.

Copy the text from the top scroll to the bottom scroll. Write a sound on each line,
e.g. t r ie d. Where the vowel spelling is split (i–e), there is a link, e.g. sh i n e.
This activity can also be used for dictation.

Book 7:   New words

Explain these words:

cast shadows – _____

cocoon – _____

leech – _____

mortal – _____

might – _____

combat – _____

Link the sentences so that they make sense:

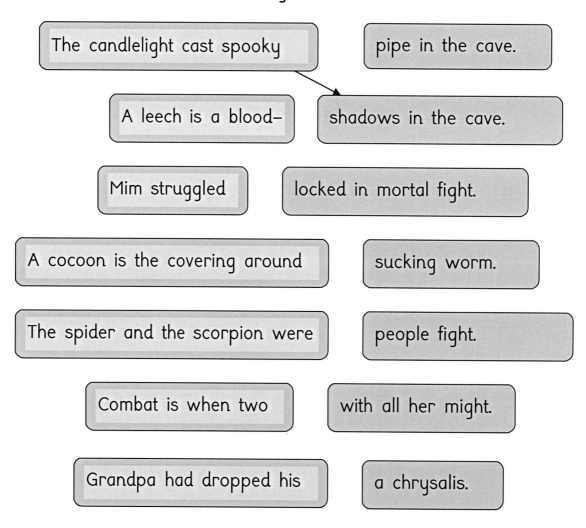

The candlelight cast spooky

pipe in the cave.

A leech is a blood–

shadows in the cave.

Mim struggled

locked in mortal fight.

A cocoon is the covering around

sucking worm.

The spider and the scorpion were

people fight.

Combat is when two

with all her might.

Grandpa had dropped his

a chrysalis.

Discuss the new words in the text and get the reader to explain them verbally and then in writing (the reader may need help with spelling). The reader can then match the two parts of the sentence.
This sheet may be photocopied by the purchaser. © Phonic Books Ltd 2014

Book 7:   Comprehension 1

The spider – what's missing?

The spider had four legs on each side. It had four ugly eyes. It had a deadly bite. The spider hid right behind a rock and waited. When Mim got stuck in the web, it climbed out from behind the rock. She got a terrible fright. She tried to break free. She cried, "I am going to die!"

Read the text above. Spot what is missing from the picture. Add it to the picture. For students who enjoy drawing, photocopy the text without the picture. Ask them to read the passage and draw a picture that fits the description. This sheet may be photocopied by the purchaser. © Phonic Books Ltd 2014

Book 7: Writing

The spider – what is it like?

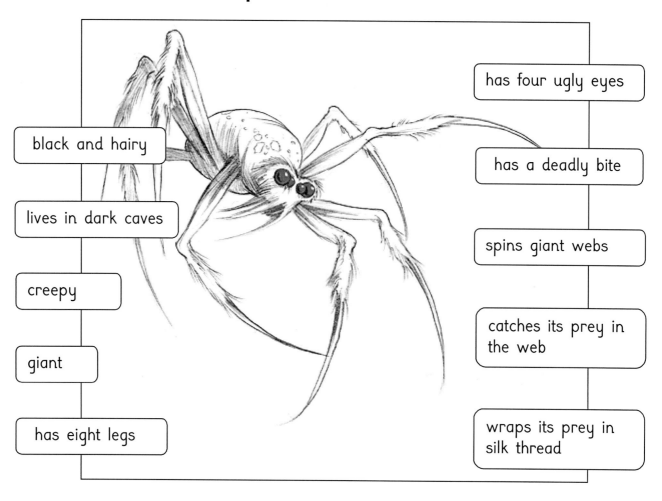

black and hairy

lives in dark caves

creepy

giant

has eight legs

has four ugly eyes

has a deadly bite

spins giant webs

catches its prey in the web

wraps its prey in silk thread

Describe the spider.

_____

_____

_____

_____

_____

_____

Describe the spider. You can use some of the words in the labels. This sheet may be photocopied by the purchaser. © Phonic Books Ltd 2014

Book 7: Comprehension 2

Scorpions – true or false?

There are 2,000 different kinds of scorpions. They live in many parts of the world. They can live in hot and cold temperatures. When they grow, their hard shell splits and a new shell grows. A scorpion has four pairs of legs. It has two claws. There are two eyes on the top of its head and 2–5 eyes on each side of its head. The tail has a sting. The sting has venom glands and a little barb that can inject the venom. Scorpions hide under rocks in the day and hunt at night. They eat small insects. Most scorpions stings are like bee stings, but some can kill humans.

Is it true?	**yes**	**no**
There are 200 kinds of scorpions.	☐	☐
Scorpions have four legs.	☐	☐
The scorpion has a barb to inject the venom.	☐	☐
Scorpions hunt in the daytime.	☐	☐
Scorpions feed on small insects.	☐	☐
Most scorpion stings kill humans.	☐	☐

Book 7: Splitting two-syllable words with 'ie' spellings

sunlight	sun	light	<u>sunlight</u>
slimy			_____
inside			_____
magpie			_____
reply			_____
spicy			_____
dryer			_____
twilight			_____
decide			_____
denied			_____
bible			_____
rely			_____
delight			_____

This activity allows the student to practice splitting two-syllable words. The teacher can use his/her own approach to splitting syllables (see page 3 for the different approaches to splitting words into syllables). These words can be used for dictation. This sheet may be photocopied by the purchaser.

Book 7:   Homophones 1: Which is which?

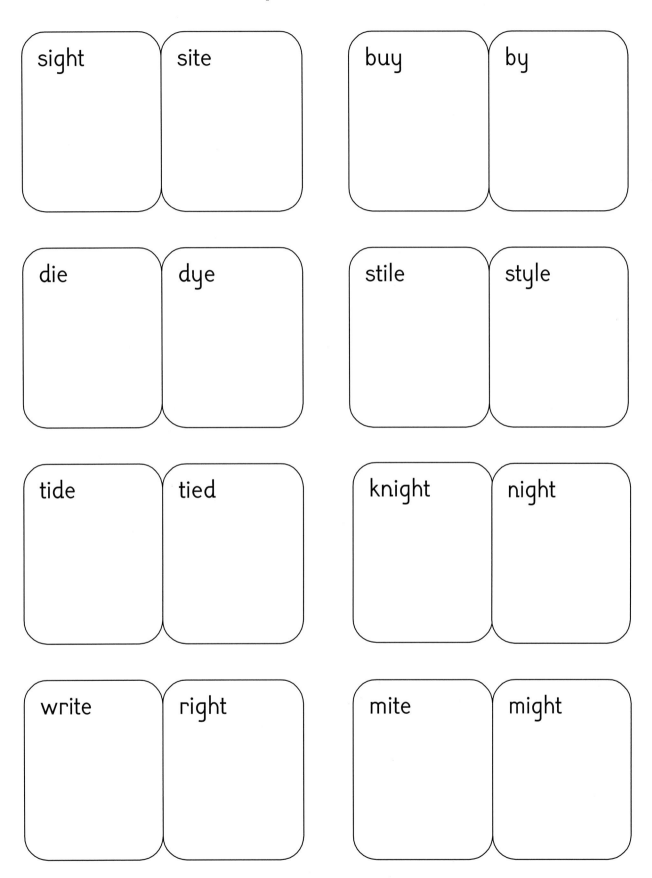

sight | site

buy | by

die | dye

stile | style

tide | tied

knight | night

write | right

mite | might

The student can draw an image on each card to help him/her remember the meaning of the word.
Photocopy the cards and play 'Concentration'. Spread the cards face down and players take turns to
find matching homophone pairs. This sheet may be photocopied by the purchaser.

Book 7: Homophones 2: Might or mite?

1. It _____ rain tomorrow.

2. I got bitten by a little _____.

3. I kick the ball with my _____ foot.

4. In the test, I had to _____ a story.

5. The girl wanted to _____ her hair black.

6. It is sad when your pets _____.

7. Every _____ we looked for shooting stars.

8. The _____ drew his sword.

9. We had to go over a _____ to reach the sheep.

10. She cut her hair into a new _____.

11. The _____ came in and everything got wet.

12. The cowboy _____ the horse to the fence.

13. At the weekend, I will _____ new shoes.

14. The car is parked _____ the toy store.

15. The blind man had lost his _____.

16. The truck dumped the bricks at the building _____.

| mite   might | die   dye | stile   style | tied   tide |
| write   right | buy   by | knight   night | sight   site |

Read the sentences above. The student can use the homophone cards from the previous page to select the correct homophone for each sentence. This sheet may be photocopied by the purchaser. © Phonic Books Ltd 2014

Book 7: Stepping stones game: 'ie'

FINISH

sky

bite

dried

slight

drive

reply

cried

final

shy

tight

hide

fried

China

strike

five

fright

spy

slimy

why

bike

fight

rind

START

lime

my

high

kite

lie

try

109

This game is for 1–4 players. Play with counters and die. This sheet may be photocopied by the purchaser. © Phonic Books Ltd 2014

Book 7: 4-in-a-row game: 'ie'

hide	might	try	lied	dine
child	dry	find	bright	pie
July	mind	fright	life	dried
idol	why	mice	time	cried
knight	slimy	thigh	revise	tie
type	ripe	blind	smile	stripe
crime	style	bible	flight	died

Play with two sets of colored counters. Two players take turns to read the word and put a counter on the word. The winner is the first to get four of his or her counters in a row. The winner places a counter on a talisman. The game is played four times until all the talismans are covered. This sheet may be photocopied by the purchaser. © Phonic Books Ltd 2014

Book 8: Attack at Nightfall

Questions for discussion

Chapter 1

  1. Where does this story take place? (p. 1)

  2. What time of day is it? Find the clue in the text. (p. 2)

Chapter 2

  1. Why does Mim think the place is haunted? (p. 4)

  2. What are the flickering lights really? (p. 5)

  3. How does Mim make a torch? (p. 6)

Chapter 3

  1. Why doesn't Mim let herself fall asleep? (p. 8)

Chapter 4

  1. What kind of bats are these? (p. 10)

  2. How did the bats torment Zak? (p. 12)

  3. Why can't the bats suck the pangolin's blood? (p. 13)

Chapter 5

  1. How does the pangolin fight off the bats? (p. 15)

  2. Why did the bats fly away? Find the clue in the text. (p. 16)

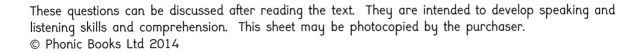

Book 8:   Blending and segmenting: aw, awe, a, al, au, ough

all	a	ll		
saw				
haunt				
fought				
walk				
small				
straw				
halt				
August				
talk				
thought				
yawn				
awe				

Blend the sounds into a word. Segment the word into sounds by writing one sound in each square.
This sheet may be photocopied by the purchaser. © Phonic Books Ltd 2014

Book 8: Reading and sorting words with aw, awe, a, al, au, ought spellings

| aw | awe | a | al |

| au | ough |

yawn	vault	tall	jaw
fought	Paul	halt	awesome
hawk	author	call	thaw
haunt	thought	stalk	draw
sought	fault	almost	haul
walk	August	claw	nought
haunt	straw	stall	paw
applaud	awe	awful	talk

Photocopy this page onto card and cut out the words. Read and sort the cards out according to the headings at the top of the page. This sheet may be photocopied by the purchaser. © Phonic Books Ltd 2014

114

Book 8: Spellings: aw, awe, a, al, au, ough

aw

awe

a

al

au

ough

Read the text in Book 8, 'Attack at Nightfall'. Find the words with aw, awe, a, al, au, ough spellings. List the words in the correct column.
This sheet may be photocopied by the purchaser. © Phonic Books Ltd 2014

Dusk fell slowly, like a black cloth drawn across the sky. "This place is haunted," Mim thought. She walked faster. "We need a torch," she said. Zak wanted to set up camp before nightfall, but Mim said they would be mauled by wild animals.

Dusk _ _ __ slowly, like a

_ _ _ _ __ cloth _ _ __ _ across

the sky. "This place is _ __ _ _ _ _,"

Mim __ ___ _. She

_ _ _ __ faster. "We need a

_ __ __," she said. Zak wanted to

_ _ _ up camp _ _ _ __

night_ _ __, but Mim said they would

be _ _ __ _ __ by _ _ _ _

_ _ _ _ _ _ _.

Copy the text from the top scroll to the bottom scroll. Write a sound on each line, e.g. f a ll. This activity can also be used for dictation. This sheet may be photocopied by the purchaser. © Phonic Books Ltd 2014

Book 8: New words

Explain these words:

bog – _____   awe – _____

dusk – _____   swarm – _____

maul – _____   torment – _____

Link the sentences so that they make sense:

A bog is an area of	flickering lights in awe.
The vampire bats came out	wet, spongy ground.
Mim was worried that they	and began to torment him.
Mim gazed at the	fangs into the pangolin's scales.
The vampire bats flew about	at dusk.
The bats landed on Zak	would be mauled by wild animals.
The bats tried to sink their small	in a swarm.

Book 8: Comprehension 1

Attack at Nightfall – what's missing?

The bats swarmed around Zak. He transformed into a

pangolin. The bats landed on the pangolin, trying to suck

its blood. But their small fangs could not get through the

hard scales. Its tail hit out with force. THUD! THUD! The

bats hit the trees.

Read the text above. Spot what is missing from the picture. Add it to the picture. For students who enjoy drawing, photocopy the text without the picture. Ask them to read the passage and draw a picture that fits the description. This sheet may be photocopied by the purchaser. © Phonic Books Ltd 2014

Book 8: Writing
The vampire bats – what are they like?

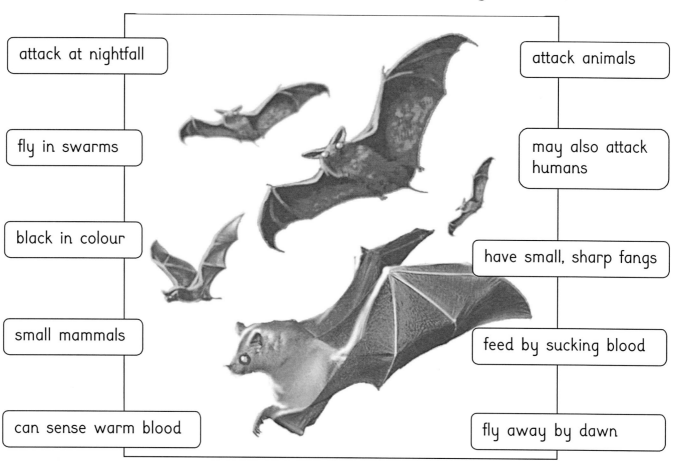

attack at nightfall

fly in swarms

black in colour

small mammals

can sense warm blood

attack animals

may also attack humans

have small, sharp fangs

feed by sucking blood

fly away by dawn

Describe the vampire bats.

_____

_____

_____

_____

_____

_____

Describe the vampire bats. You can use some of the words in the labels. This sheet may be photocopied by the purchaser. © Phonic Books Ltd 2014

Book 8: Comprehension 2

Vampire bats – true or false?

Vampire bats can be found in Mexico, Brazil, Chile and Argentina. Unlike fruit-eating bats, vampire bats feed on blood. They have short muzzles with special sensors that can locate blood. Vampire bats have razor-sharp teeth. They can even shave the fur off an animal. They cut the skin of an animal (usually a sleeping mammal or bird) and lap up the blood when it bleeds. Their saliva has a special chemical that stops the blood from clotting. Vampire bats hunt at night. They often live in dark places and fly out in large groups. Occasionally, they feed on human blood.

Is it true?	yes	no
Vampire bats eat fruit.	☐	☐
They locate blood with the sensors in their noses.	☐	☐
They suck the blood of an animal.	☐	☐
Their saliva keeps the blood flowing.	☐	☐
Vampire bats fly out in the daytime.	☐	☐
They mostly feed on human blood.	☐	☐

Read the text. Now read the sentences below and put a check in the boxes according to whether they are true or false. This sheet may be photocopied by the purchaser.
© Phonic Books Ltd 2014

Book 8: Splitting two-syllable words with aw, awe, a, al, au, ough spellings

word			
awful	aw	ful	<u>awful</u>
awesome			_____
almost			_____
applaud			_____
haunted			_____
author			_____
thoughtful			_____
talking			_____
walking			_____
smaller			_____
calling			_____
August			_____
lawful			_____

This activity allows the student to practice splitting two-syllable words. The teacher can use his/her own approach to splitting syllables (see page 3 for the different approaches to splitting words into syllables). These words can be used for dictation. This sheet may be photocopied by the purchaser.

Book 8:   Homophones 1: Which is which?

maul	mall	bald	bawled
taught	taut	paws	pause
	all	awl	
ball	bawl	hall	haul

The student can draw an image on each card to help him/her remember the meaning of the word. Photocopy the cards and play 'Concentration'. Spread the cards face down and players take turns to find matching homophone pairs. This sheet may be photocopied by the purchaser.

Book 8: Homophones 2: Mall or maul?

1. If you want to buy sneakers, go to the _____.

2. You must not go near the lion. It will _____ you.

3. The suspect had a _____ head under his hat.

4. The baby _____ because she was hungry.

5. The rope had to be _____ to tow the car.

6. My grandma _____ me to read.

7. The dog's _____ were covered in mud.

8. After a short _____, the program continued.

9. _____ the children clapped loudly.

10. An _____ is a tool for making holes.

11. He kicked the _____ over the fence.

12. The tears started and she began to _____ her eyes out.

13. We had to _____ the piano up the stairs.

14. We keep the bicycles in the _____.

hall haul   maul mall   bald bawled   paws pause

all awl   taut taught   ball bawl

Read the sentences above. The student can use the homophone cards from the previous page to select the correct homophone for each sentence. This sheet may be photocopied by the purchaser. © Phonic Books Ltd 2014

Book 8: Stepping stones game: aw, awe, a, al, au, ough

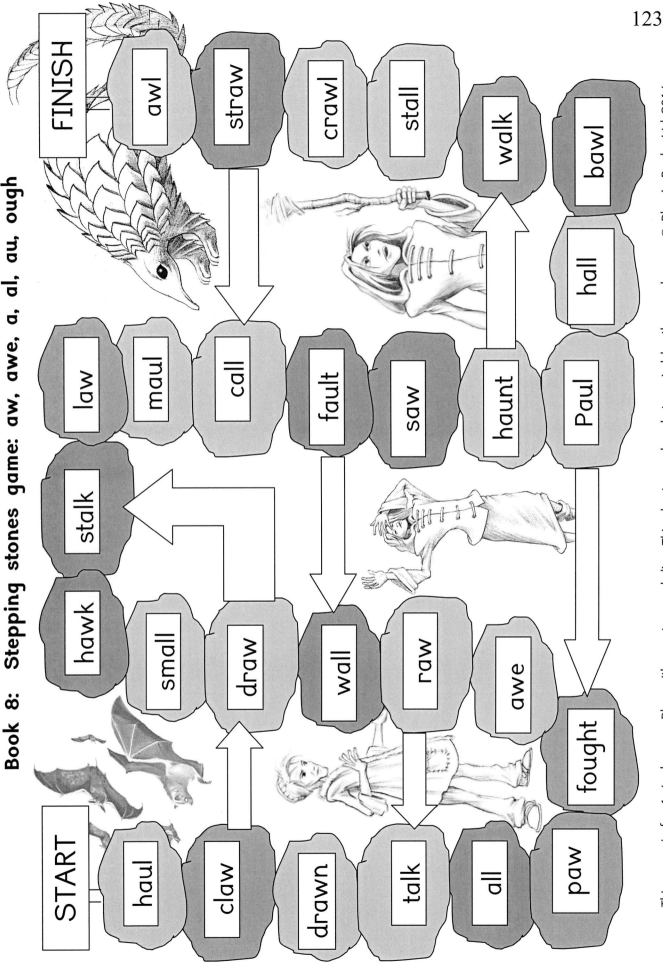

FINISH

awl

straw

crawl

stall

walk

bawl

hall

Paul

haunt

law

maul

call

fault

saw

stalk

hawk

small

draw

wall

raw

awe

fought

START

haul

claw

drawn

talk

all

paw

123

Book 8: 4-in-a-row game: aw, awe, a, al, au, ough

bawl	fall	hawk	wall	jaw
stalk	pawn	walk	awl	author
stall	crawl	fault	ball	claw
dawn	fought	awe	lawn	tall
straw	small	haunt	draw	fraud
awful	halt	launch	call	all
paw	raw	hall	talk	fawn

Play with two sets of colored counters. Two players take turns to read the word and put a counter on the word. The winner is the first to get four of his or her counters in a row. The winner places a counter on a talisman. The game is played four times until all the talismans are covered. This sheet may be photocopied by the purchaser. © Phonic Books Ltd 2014

Book 9: Mountain Scare

Questions for discussion

Chapter 1

   1. Why does Mim say 'the air is thin up here'? (p. 1)

   2. What does 'Zak lost his footing' mean? (p. 2)

Chapter 2

   1. Why is the chapter called 'Some Helpful Advice'? (p. 3)

   2. Why was there a chill in the air? (p. 5)

Chapter 3

   1. What did Zak dare Mim to do? (p. 6)

   2. Why did Mim think the cave was an animal's lair? (p. 8)

Chapter 4

   1. Why do Zak and Mim sit by the fire in grim silence?

(p. 9)

   2. Why do the hairs on Zak's neck stand up? (p. 10)

Chapter 5

   1. How did the bear survive the werewolves? (p. 16)

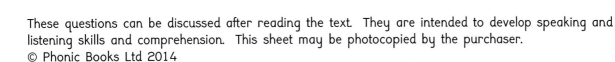

Book 9: Blending and segmenting: air, are, ear, ere, eir

word						
fair	f	air				
care						
their						
pear						
chair						
share						
where						
swear						
stair						
spare						
beware						
careless						
werewolf						

Blend the sounds into a word. Segment the word into sounds by writing one sound in each square. Segmenting words into sounds may vary according to regional pronunciation. This sheet may be photocopied by the purchaser. © Phonic Books Ltd 2014

Book 9: Reading and sorting words with air, are, ear, ere, eir spellings

air	are	ear	ere	eir

pair	blare	wear	there
heir	lair	stare	bear
mare	flair	tear	dare
where	their	bare	pear
spare	affair	fair	declare
despair	care	stair	impair
hare	glare	Clair	fairly
fare	chair	rare	swear

Photocopy this page onto card and cut out the words. Read and sort the cards out according to the headings at the top of the page. This sheet may be photocopied by the purchaser. © Phonic Books Ltd 2014

128

Book 9: Spellings: air, are, ear, ere, eir

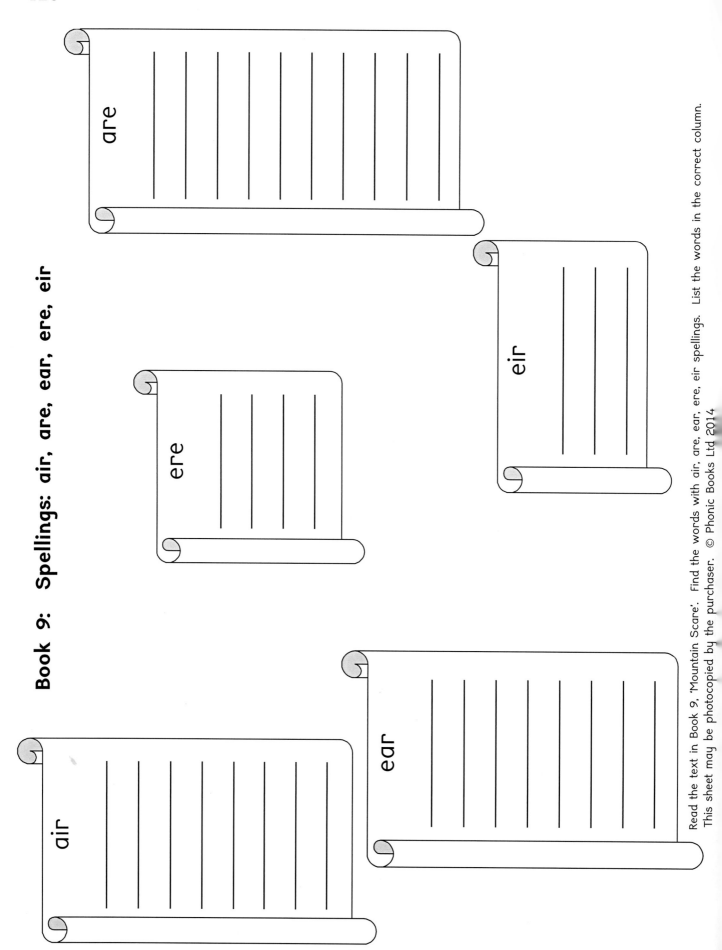

are

ere

eir

air

ear

Read the text in Book 9, 'Mountain Scare'. Find the words with air, are, ear, ere, eir spellings. List the words in the correct column.
This sheet may be photocopied by the purchaser. © Phonic Books Ltd 2014

Book 9: Reading and spelling

Mim went into the cave. There was a smell of dog in the air. Was this an animal's lair? She was not aware of two yellow eyes staring at her. "There's nothing in the cave," she declared, but she didn't dare go any further into the cave.

Mim _ _ _ _ into the cave. __ ___ was a _ _ _ __ of _ _ _ in the ___. Was __ _ _ an animal's _ ___? She was not _ _ ___ of two yellow eyes staring at her. "__ ___'s nothing in the cave," she declared, but she didn't _ ___ go any further into the cave.

Copy the text in the top scroll to the bottom scroll. Write a sound on each line, e.g. f air.
This activity can also be used for dictation. Segmenting words into sounds may vary according to regional pronunciation. This sheet may be photocopied by the purchaser.
© Phonic Books Ltd 2014

Book 9: New words

Explain these words:

glared – _____   to inch – _____

footing – _____   lair – _____

ledge – _____   scramble – _____

Link the sentences so that they make sense:

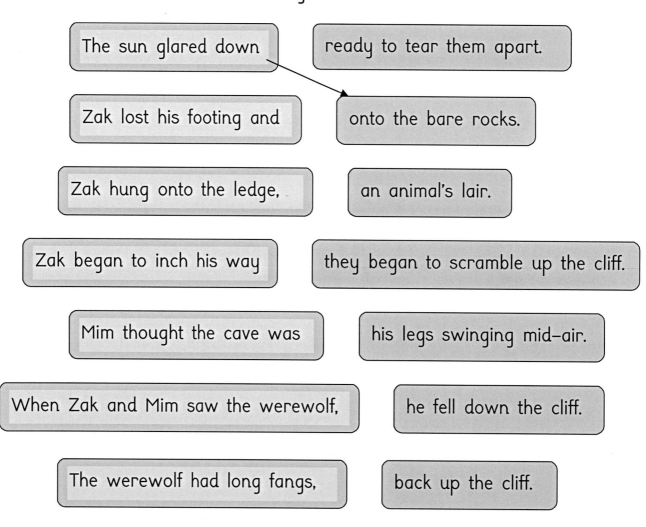

The sun glared down

ready to tear them apart.

Zak lost his footing and

onto the bare rocks.

Zak hung onto the ledge,

an animal's lair.

Zak began to inch his way

they began to scramble up the cliff.

Mim thought the cave was

his legs swinging mid–air.

When Zak and Mim saw the werewolf,

he fell down the cliff.

The werewolf had long fangs,

back up the cliff.

Discuss the new words in the text and get the reader to explain them verbally and then in writing (the reader may need help with spelling). The reader can then match the two parts of the sentence.

Book 9:   Comprehension 1

Nightfall – what's missing?

The sun went down. There was a chill in the air.

The shadows fell over the bare rocks. Soon the

moon sailed up into the sky. Zak and Mim sat

hunched by the campfire. "I can't bear the cold,"

Mim said. The pair of them sat staring into the

black night, shivering.

Read the text above. Spot what is missing from the picture. Add it to the picture. For students who enjoy drawing, photocopy the text without the picture. Ask them to read the passage and draw a picture that fits the description. This sheet may be photocopied by the purchaser. © Phonic Books Ltd 2014

Book 9: Writing

The werewolves – what are they like?

part man, part wolf

appear at full moon

very strong

attack in a pack

long claws

pointed ears

yellow eyes

sharp fangs

bite and scratch

will turn humans into werewolves

cannot bear daylight

Describe the werewolves.

_____

_____

_____

_____

_____

_____

_____

Describe the werewolves. You can use some of the words in the labels. This sheet may be photocopied by the purchaser. © Phonic Books Ltd 2014

Book 9: Comprehension 2

Werewolves – true or false?

Hundreds of years ago, people in Europe had a great fear of wolves. A myth about werewolves grew from that fear. People believed that werewolves were men who changed from humans to werewolves when the full moon came out. Then they would turn back into human form. People believed that a man would turn into a werewolf if he had been scratched or bitten by other werewolves. Werewolves had superhuman strength and could rip a human apart. People feared that werewolves lived secretly among them. If they suspected that someone was a werewolf, that person would be put to death.

Is it true?	yes	no
Today, people in Europe have a great fear of wolves.	☐	☐
Werewolves are not real. They are a myth.	☐	☐
If a man became a werewolf, he would stay that way.	☐	☐
Werewolves appear only when the sun is out.	☐	☐
Werewolves were stronger than humans.	☐	☐
People were afraid that werewolves lived around them.	☐	☐

Read the text. Now read the sentences below and put a check in the boxes according to whether they are true or false. This sheet may be photocopied by the purchaser. © Phonic Books Ltd 2014

Book 9: Splitting two-syllable words with air, are, ear, ere, eir spellings

word	syllable 1	syllable 2	answer
fairly	fair	ly	<u>fairly</u>
beware			_____
nowhere			_____
farewell			_____
despair			_____
affair			_____
careless			_____
rarely			_____
heirloom			_____
hairless			_____
repair			_____
declare			_____
footwear			_____

This activity allows the student to practice splitting two-syllable words. The teacher can use his/her own approach to splitting syllables (see page 3 for the different approaches to splitting words into syllables). These words can be used for dictation. This sheet may be photocopied by the purchaser.

Book 9:   Homophones 1: Which is which?

air	heir

fair	fare

pear	pair

bear	bare

stare	stair

wear	where

hair	hare

there	their

The student can draw an image on each card to help him/her remember the meaning of the word.
Photocopy the cards and play pelmanism. This sheet may be photocopied by the purchaser.
© Phonic Books Ltd 2014

1.   I didn't have enough money for the bus _____.

2.   I won the stuffed animal at the _____ .

3.   The _____ was very thin on the mountain peak.

4.   The prince was the _____ to the throne.

5.   The kids wrote _____ names on _____ bags.

6.   Once upon a time, _____ were three bears.

7.   _____ did you put the car keys?

8.   It was so cold, we had to _____ hats and gloves.

9.   We had to pack an extra _____ of shoes.

10.   The _____ tree has lots of fruit this year.

11.   The _____ stood in the river to catch fish.

12.   The sharp rocks cut into his _____ feet.

13.   It is rude to _____.

14.   Mom tripped on the _____s and hurt her leg.

15.   I am growing my _____ long.

16.   The _____ darted across the field, into the bush.

| air   heir | fair   fare | pear   pair | bear   bare |
| stare   stair | wear   where | hair   hare | there   their |

Book 9: Stepping stones game: air, are, ear, ere, eir

START

air

bare

there

heir

pear

chair

ware

their

wear

flare

where

care

stair

fare

beware

lair

scare

tear

mare

Clair

fair

spare

FINISH

declare

swear

repair

share

bear

despair

Book 9:   4-in-a-row game: air, are, ear, ere, eir

dare	fair	there	pear	heir
air	care	flair	glare	pair
repair	bear	hair	stare	fare
chair	share	where	their	lair
wear	ware	pare	swear	tear
stair	hare	mare	scare	affair
blare	rare	dairy	snare	spare

Play with two sets of colored counters. Two players take turns to read the word and put a counter on the word. The winner is the first to get four of his or her counters in a row. The winner places a counter on a talisman. The game is played four times until all the talismans are covered. This sheet may be photocopied by the purchaser. © Phonic Books Ltd 2014

Book 10: The Dark Master

Questions for discussion

Chapter 1

   1. What are turrets and arches? (p. 1)

   2. Why did Mim's heart sink when she saw the gate? (p. 3)

Chapter 2

   1. Who do you think sent the large bird? (p. 5)

Chapter 3

   1. How did Zak get into the castle? (p. 7)

   2. Why do you think the Dark Master kept Grandpa and Mim

      captive in the glass tower? (p. 8)

Chapter 4

   1. Why does the Dark Master want the talisman? (p. 9)

   2. Why did Zak agree to hand over the talisman? (p. 11)

   3. Why do you think the talisman did not break in half? (p. 12)

Chapter 5

   1. If you were to write the next book, what would happen in it?

      (p. 16)

Book 10: Blending and segmenting: ar

word					
art	ar	t			
carve					
march					
bark					
dart					
arch					
hard					
start					
shark					
alarm					
army					
parking					
sharpen					

Blend the sounds into a word. Segment the word into sounds by writing one sound in each square. Segmenting words into sounds may vary according to regional pronunciation. This sheet may be photocopied by the purchaser. © Phonic Books Ltd 2014

Book 10: Reading and sorting words with ar spelling

ar as in art	ar as in vary	ar as in warm

charm	wary	swarm	dart
harsh	yard	scary	wart
dark	arches	alarm	army
daring	stars	warn	march
staring	stark	large	war
warble	sharp	caring	harm
shark	arch	start	warthog
warlord	paring	artist	carp

Photocopy this page onto card and cut out the words. Read and sort the cards out according to sounds of the ar spelling. This sheet may be photocopied by the purchaser.
© Phonic books Ltd 2014

Book 10: Spelling: ar

Words with ar spelling

Page number

Read the text in Book 10, 'The Dark Master'. Find the words with ar spellings. Write the words in the left column and page number you found them on in the right column. This sheet may be photocopied by the purchaser.

Book 10: Reading and spelling

Mim looked at the barbed gates. Her heart sank. "It's like a fortress, but we've come too far to give up now," she said. This was her chance. Mim heard her heart beating fast. She tried to stay calm.

Mim looked at the _ __ _ __ gates.

Her heart _ _ _ _.

"It's like a _ __ _ _ _ __, but we've

come too _ __ to give _ _ now,"

she said. __ _ _ was her

__ _ _ __. Mim heard her

heart _ __ _ _ __ _ _ _ _.

She _ _ __ _ to _ _ __ calm.

Copy the text in the top scroll to the bottom scroll. Write a sound on each line, e.g. p ar t.
This activity can also be used for dictation. This sheet may be photocopied by the purchaser.
© Phonic Books Ltd 2014

144

Book 10: New words

Explain these words:

vast   – _____   darted – _____

turret   – _____   talons – _____

barbed   – _____   rap   – _____

Link the sentences so that they make sense:

Zak and Mim saw a vast castle	grabbed Mim with its talons.
When Mim saw the barbed gate,	in the valley.
The large bird swooped down and	her heart sank.
Zak darted from rock to rock because	a manticore.
A turret is a small	he wanted Zak to listen to him.
Grandpa rapped on the glass because	tower in a castle.
The Dark Master turned into	he did not want to get caught.

Discuss the new words in the text and get the reader to explain them verbally and then in writing (the reader may need help with spelling). The reader can then match the two parts of the sentence.
This sheet may be photocopied by the purchaser. © Phonic Books Ltd 2014

Book 10:   Comprehension 1

The Dark Master – what's missing?

"At last you have come to give me the talisman!"

laughed the Dark Master. His face was a black

mask. Zak held the talisman in the palm of his hand.

He looked calmly at the Dark Master. "Half the

talisman for Grandpa and half for Mim," he said.

Spot the missing detail in the picture. Add it to the picture.   For students who enjoy
drawing, photocopy the text without the picture. Ask them to read the passage and draw a
picture that fits the description. This sheet may be photocopied by the purchaser.

Book 10: Writing

The manticore – what is it like?

has body of a lion

is red in colour

has wings like a giant bat

has a club on the end of his tail

can shoot darts from his tail

has yellow eyes

has sharp teeth

has pointed ears

eats human flesh

his face is like the Dark Master's face

Describe the manticore.

_____

_____

_____

_____

_____

_____

_____

Describe the manticore. You can use some of the words in the labels. This sheet may be photocopied by the purchaser. © Phonic Books Ltd 2014

Book 10: Comprehension 2

Manticore – true or false?

A manticore is a fierce creature from legends. The word 'manticore' comes from Greek and means 'man–eater'. This is because people believed the manticore liked to eat human flesh. The manticore has the body of a red lion and a human head. Some legends say that it has blue eyes. It has three rows of sharp teeth, which look like shark's teeth. The manticore has a trumpet–like voice. In some stories, it has horns and wings. The manticore can have a tail like a dragon or a scorpion. It can shoot poisonous spines from its tail. These spines can kill or paralyze its victims. Many years ago, people believed that manticores really existed.

Is it true?	yes	no
The word manticore comes from Greek.	☐	☐
A manticore has a lion's head and the body of a man.	☐	☐
A manticore and a shark have the same kind of teeth.	☐	☐
All manticores have horns and wings.	☐	☐
Manticores kill humans to eat their flesh.	☐	☐
Nobody really believed that manticores existed.	☐	☐

Read the text. Now read the sentences below and put a check in the boxes according to whether they are true or false. This sheet may be photocopied by the purchaser.

Book 10: Splitting two-syllable words with ar

charming	charm	ing		charming
harmful				_____
artist				_____
parking				_____
started				_____
largest				_____
charging				_____
army				_____
darkness				_____
darted				_____
arches				_____
guarding				_____
parchment				_____

This activity allows the student to practice splitting two-syllable words. The teacher can use his/her own approach to splitting syllables (see page 3 for the different approaches to splitting words into syllables). These words can be used for dictation. This sheet may be photocopied by the purchaser.

Book 10: Stepping stones game: ar

149

START

art · harp · cart · alarm · start · farm

hard · spark · lark · barber · arch · park · sharp

shark · marsh · carp · tart · stars · part · army · charm · mark

FINISH · ark · harder · darts · march · artist · barter

This game is for 1–4 players. Play with counters and die. This sheet may be photocopied by the purchaser. © Phonic Books Ltd 2014

Book 10: 4-in-a-row game: ar

cart	arch	artist	party	mark
parts	barn	shark	alarm	starve
start	carve	sharp	farm	harm
spark	carp	park	darts	ark
army	stars	card	harp	yard
starch	guard	dark	harsh	scar
bar	afar	starch	ajar	marsh

Play with two sets of colored counters. Two players take turns to read any word and put a counter on it. The winner is the first to get four of his or her counters in a row. The winner places a counter on a talisman. The game is played four times until all the talismans are covered. This sheet may be photocopied by the purchaser. © Phonic Books Ltd 2014